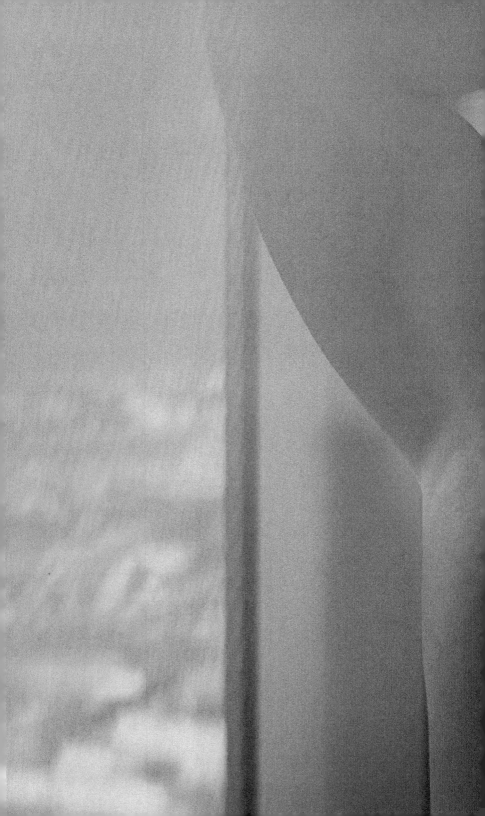

Off LIMITS

USA TODAY BESTSELLING AUTHOR
SUSANA MOHEL

Off Limits by Susana Mohel
Copyright © 2020 Susana Mohel
Cover design by Sue C. Hoffman
Cover picture: Kamil Majdanski
Editing by Griffin Editing Services & Lucia ToMe
Proofreading by Virginia Tesy-Carey

This one goes out to the one I love.

—S

"Woman is sacred; the woman one loves is holy."

—Alexandre Dumas, The Count of Monte Cristo

Playlist

In the End – Linkin Park
Nothing Else Matters – Metallica
The sound of Silence – Disturbed
Thick Skin – Leona Lewis
Brown Eyed Girl – Van Morrison
Legacy – Eminem
Again – Lenny Kravitz
The Reason - Hoobastank
Madness – Muse
Bird Set Free – Sia
Writing's on The Wall – Sam Smith
Thunderstruck – AC/DC
Feelings – Maroon five
Amazed – Lonestar

Prologue

Many kids say they learned by example, dreaming of being a great man, like the one that raised them. My grandfather filled that role, with so much love, and a few pennies in his pocket, he showed me the path. My goal was to be an honorable man just like him.

My options were very limited, but that never made me lose focus. Becoming a scoundrel, a womanizer, and a good for nothing was not what I wanted for my life, so while the boys at my school wasted time with girls and parties, I mapped out my future.

On the back of an empty notebook I wrote the rules that would seal my fate.

Yes, because I would forge a name, one that was not linked to debts or scams.

To this day I have followed those rules to the T, they have taken me to where I am now, and they have also put me in front of the greatest challenge

I'm determined to achieve it, not only because it is a challenge, but because when you know something is worth it, you risk everything in order to keep it.

I'm Adrik Houston and I'm ready to fight for the woman who was born in the fire of a storm.

Rule # 1: May your actions always reflect who you are and what you believe in. Loyalty begins when you are true to yourself.

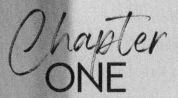

Chapter ONE

"But that is humiliating," I tell my father, rising from my chair and walking along the carpet of the office. I'm sure the air conditioning is on full blast, but I'm sweating like a pig.

Suddenly the walls full of photos, books, and other memorabilia are overwhelming me. I hate it. I hate feeling small and helpless.

My father stares at me, his brown eyes so similar to mine, it's almost like staring into a mirror. Except that he looks a little like Burt Reynolds, minus the mustache.

"It's the opportunity you've been waiting for, Jordan, you should be thanking me for it," he adds loudly, as if he's offering me a gift from heaven.

And that makes my temperature rise, I feel like I am about to erupt, like a volcano.

"What should I thank you for?" I ask, trying not to raise my voice. God knows how much effort it's taking me. "My father using all of his connections to get me an offering for a posting that I don't even want or qualify for?"

"Of course you qualify," he replies, as if it were obvious. "And it will lead you to a brilliant future, kid."

For the first time in all my years of duty as an officer of the US Navy, I feel that the uniform is way too big for me.

This news just diminishes me to an insignificant rag doll, whose father moves her at his complete discretion. All my efforts and years serving have gone down the tube.

He's screwed me.

My father has screwed me.

"We both know that's not true." Let's at least be honest here, no point in lies or half-truths. "I don't have the service time, I'm missing a couple of years to complete them and…"

"Are you questioning my judgment, Lieutenant?"

Shit, he pulled his superior's card out.

This is a fight that I will lose. I live in a world of rules that I can't break.

Or at least, I have chosen not to.

"Dad, you know that what I'm saying is true." I can play this game too, and even if logic is the last card in my deck, I still have to try it.

"I'm your superior, so don't fuck with me. You will do whatever I order you to."

If we start arguing, this isn't going to go well.

The day that had been going just fine has now gone to hell. Murphy's Law is not wrong, ladies and gentlemen, I knew it was too good to be true that my sailors followed all of my instructions perfectly and that even the wind was collaborating with me.

I can feel my heart drumming in my ears. Better to laugh than mess with him, I prefer it to ending up screaming at him, or even worse, beating him. Imagine the headlines, '*United States Navy officer beats her father in a fight, her father a decorated Admiral.*'

"You are my father when it suits you, but I'm never sure who I am speaking to, my father or the scary officer."

His face turns red, we Zanettis are hot-blooded folks. Our Italian heritage means we don't like to be contradicted. Unfortunately for my father, I also like to have my way.

After all, I'm his only daughter. And we are very similar.

"I'm always going to look after your interests, never doubt that," he admits with a tone that to innocent ears, might even sound conciliatory.

Of course my father watches over my interests. In his own way.

"My interests?" I argue, resisting the urge to shout, bearing in mind that we are in the base commander's office, not at home and I'm sure the room isn't soundproofed. My father being my superior makes things difficult, and I have to remind myself that my family isn't like any other family. "Tell me, then, why is it good for my career to make a fool of myself in front of the sailors I'm in charge of?"

I've spent years setting my own goals, trusting my own instinct to survive in the open fight that is the real world.

"Jordan, nobody is talking about handing you the badges in cereal boxes, you will still have to compete, work hard, and strive to earn them."

"I've done that ever since I was admitted to the academy," I shout, no longer giving a shit who can hear me. "I have worked very hard, day by day to make myself a place, to earn respect for what I do, not for bearing the last name Zanetti."

"You should be thankful, many would like to be in your place."

I haven't seen my father in more than six months, as he spends most of his time in his fancy office in Washington, and I have been stationed in Pearl Harbor – Hickam. When they told me that he was coming to the base to see me, I was very happy. All my life it's been me and him against the world.

Now we are against each other.

"Then choose one of your other pawns and offer them the incentive. I don't want it."

"The decision has already been made," he says, patting the smooth wood of the desk. "The orders have been delivered and there is no going back."

And knowing what the people in my unit are like, surely the gossip has already run like fire over a barrel of gunpowder.

"You're going to go far," he adds as if it were by divine intervention. "Look at me, the son of a construction worker and a secretary. If I was capable of becoming an admiral, you will reach even higher goals. The pentagon awaits you."

My father has a fair point, I wasn't born to be average. I'm one in a million.

But this is not what I want. My interests are different, I am more interested in research and knowing how things work, that's why I studied engineering in college. While my father wanted me to choose law or something that would put me on the command line, I chose to be a restricted line officer.

Being the progeny of Admiral Zanetti has not always being a blessing, at least not here. My father is steering the helm away from the destiny that I had planned.

"You were born to be in command, Jordan, to be on top of the world."

"This is not fair," I respond automatically without realizing it, almost thinking out loud. "I want to be part of E.D.O., not a combat officer."

Yes, an Engineering Duty Officer, to my father's disappointment. Ever since high school when I discovered how curious I am, always wanting to know how stuff works and make it better, I knew there was no better place for me than the

US Navy. I'd always wanted to be here, but that gave me a new reason to join.

"Military life is not fair sometimes, it's not about what you want, it's about following orders without questioning them. You will take the place assigned to you and that is all."

"I don't think that…"

He makes a face of disgust, as he straightens his back, becoming the relentless commander that everyone obeys.

"Here we go again. You are not paid to think, Lieutenant, you are here to serve."

Damn my luck. I have worked like a mule from day one, and this is not the way I expected to receive incentives. I should have known the fact that my father and I are on the same base was never going to bring anything good.

Hawaii, the archipelago that many call paradise, has now become my personal hell.

Even though I enjoy living here.

"Get ready, because on Monday you travel to San Diego. NBSD will be your new home. You have already been assigned lodging at the base, everything is ready for you. If you need help with moving, I can help you get a moving company."

God, my head is spinning, what I need is a good excuse to get out of all this.

"My men are in full training; you know that we're about to leave for the Middle East and there is so much I still need to do."

I'm pleading my case, trying to find an excuse but I know I'm fighting a losing battle. My destiny is already cast.

"They will still leave," my father clarifies. "But there are other plans for you. Take the weekend off to prepare. It's Thursday, see you Monday on the tarmac at six hundred."

I would really like to set this damn office on fire caring very little about all the beautiful maps adorning the walls that will end up as ashes. The hundreds of books on the wooden shelves would only help the office burn until there was nothing left. The worst thing is, although I don't like the imposition, I have no choice but to obey his orders.

I always knew this was going to happen at some point, but I never imagined it would be so soon. I guess it was only a matter of time before my father would use his influence to get me to follow the path he has so carefully set for me.

Because I had the audacity to be born a girl. Not the precious son he was praying for.

My mother died after giving birth and my father never got married again, so Admiral Zanetti had to be satisfied with me.

Like I said before, it's him and I. He is all the family I have.

"Do you have anything else to tell me, Admiral?"

"Sit down, Jordania, we have to talk."

I remain standing where I am, staring into his eyes. I can't challenge him the way I would like to, but I'm not going to be his puppet either.

"Am I going to talk to my father or to Admiral Zanetti?" I ask.

My father raises an eyebrow in a gesture of displeasure, and I must contain the smile that starts appearing on my face. He is angry, very angry, and that gives me a strange feeling of satisfaction.

I drop into the chair, without taking my eyes off his. I don't care if this seems unprofessional, this is a family matter, and no one can tell me otherwise.

If I was any other person, I would not be in such a disastrous situation.

"Jordan, this is a great opportunity for you. There is only one position available so the competition is going to be tough, but I am certain that you will succeed. That place belongs to you."

"For being the offspring of the illustrious Giordano Zanetti," I challenge him.

"Don't act like a brat, Jordania," he snaps. "My name is respected."

"Then you should know how important mine is *to me!*"

"Even if you refuse to recognize it, you and I will always be family, so stop being so stubborn. You were born for great things, daughter."

And that is my sentence. My downfall.

"I'm going to do what I have to do, there is no doubt about that."

And I will do it, all my years of hard work are not going to go to hell.

I just have to think about how I'm going to deal with it.

"That's all I wanted to hear. I know you won't let me down."

"This is not about you, I want to make that clear."

"In the end the result is the same." He smiles smugly. "Now, you may leave, Lieutenant."

I head out of the office, carefully closing the door, even though I'd love to slam it like a rebellious brat. But once again, I have to remind myself that he might be my father, but we are inside a naval base, where he is my superior officer. If I tried to do anything of that nature I will be subpoenaed by internal affairs before I could even walk two steps.

Like it or not, Giordano Zanetti is my superior and as such, I must respect him, obey him, and never question his orders.

Semper Fortis; always strong. How complicated it is sometimes.

Fortunately, I don't see anyone on my way out. I need a moment of peace to put my thoughts in order and mentally prepare for what will follow.

This has changed my plans radically. Until a few hours ago, I thought I would be leaving for the Persian Gulf, as second in command of a destroyer. Now I have to leave that plan behind, and pack my things to go to a destination I had not expected.

I'm going to the mainland to pursue a dream that isn't mine.

The pentagon. I'm not interested in any of that, the nightmare of dealing with politicians, the bureaucracy isn't my jam, politics doesn't interest me in the slightest.

I don't want to see life go by through the window, I just want to live by my own rules.

I want to join in and play, not be a spectator.

Why couldn't I be interested in something else?

Medicine, architecture. Hell, even obstetrics for chickens sounds attractive right now.

Anything else.

But no, here I am, because ever since I can remember, my father has used his rank to control me. First I went to a boarding school, then I went straight to Annapolis. The Naval Academy is such an intensively demanding program, as soon as I set foot in there I was determined to become one of the top three Midshipmen in my plebe year. I earned respect doing my best.

For many sailors, the sea is only their place of work, they stop seeing it as the wonder that it is. For me it is something else. It's my home. I love surfing, sailing, but I'm not interested in commanding a warship. I just want to make them better.

Fucking shit, I wish I could just buy a sailboat and get thrown offshore.

I have discovered that being in the Navy is not just a profession, it's a lifestyle, a religion. And I became a fervent believer, I like its values, its goals, the way it turns ordinary men and women into titans.

Never in my life have I wanted to be someone else.

Until now my heart has always been full of pride, I never felt I was in the wrong place or time.

Until now…

I keep walking on the dock, between two aircraft carriers stationed there. As I get to the end of the platform, I want to sit there with my legs hanging feeling the salty water. But I can't. I'm wearing the service uniform.

I'm here, alone although I'm surrounded by people. I put my hand on my mouth, muffling the sobs threatening to go out, the other over my chest. My heart and stomach hurting.

Like an unexpected storm, this is devastating me. The most important things in my life are colliding. My father, the only family I have left, is threatening the career I've been working on since leaving high school. Eons ago. Or at least, I feel it that way.

Tears are running down my face while thinking about this place that has been my home for almost five years. I've learned to love these islands, the people here are amazing. I start to cry even harder as I realize I won't be here to enjoy the New Year's Eve fireworks. After seeing the display in Hawaii, everything else seems like a bad light show. I feel like I am being cast away from heaven, and how much I will miss everything, from the beautiful beaches to the small things like shave ice. I close my eyes and lift my chin, letting the salt breeze calm me down, as it always does. It is an elixir, a balm. My lullaby.

I let myself be seduced by the sea. I wish I could take my hat off and let down my long, dark hair. But I can't. While wearing the service uniform, I must follow the rules.

What I want doesn't matter.

Breathe, Jordania. Just breathe.

The magic seems to have stopped working.

I am like an energy charged cloud ready to collide with the first thing that comes in front of it.

"Lieutenant," I hear a voice shouting in the distance.

I don't care, it's not for me, there must be plenty more officers of my rank swarming around.

"Lieutenant Jordania Zanetti," he shouts again, this time closer, just a few steps behind me.

I refuse to believe it, but the voice is insistent and I can't help turning.

"Jordan? Didi!"

We are at the base, why does he call me that?

"What are you doing here?" It's the first thing that comes out of my mouth.

"Is that the way to welcome your best friend?" he says smiling, opening his arms as if we were to hug. "Don't make that sour face, you know I'm here to support you, always."

He's absolutely right. Although time has passed, he and I have always been two peas in a pod. Partners in crime. I think his mother is still waiting for us to fall in love and give her grandbabies to spoil.

"Casper, what are you doing here?"

I really do not need to ask, I already know the answer.

This might be United States Navy, but sometimes it seems as if I were in a schoolyard.

Gossip spreads faster than the wind.

"You found out, right?"

My friend nods while looking at me, muttering a curse.

Rule # 2: Once you have a target, trace a plan. Defeat comes for the unprepared.

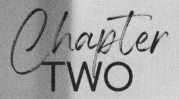

Chapter TWO

I spill my guts to my friend. I tell him everything. From the orders I've received, to the discussion with my father. He knows him well, not only because my father's name is well known within the force, but because he has spent some holidays with us, in the house my father has in Cape Cod.

"What do you think about all of this?" I ask.

He gives me a sad smile. "What I think is not important, Didi, since the decision is a done deal. Leaving aside what people will say, it's a great opportunity, so why not take advantage of it? You've been through a lot and nobody deserves it more than you."

My past has nothing to do with this.

Not even the mistakes I made. I've left those on the other side of the ocean.

"What have you heard?" That's what I really want to know, I'm not interested in cheap psychology.

"Some are saying they only gave it to you because you're the daughter of Admiral Zanetti, while others say that you're the jewel of the base, the golden girl of the force," he replies. "But since I'm your best friend, I told everyone that because your experience is exceptional, you were always going to be fast-tracked. Everyone knows how impressive you've been since you were in the academy. No one has a better record than you, daughter of the admiral or not."

I have no idea why his words bother me. I know that my friend did it with the best of intentions, however, his actions leave a bittersweet taste.

Why the fuck should I need someone to defend me?

"Thank you for your support, Cas," I answer in a neutral voice.

"You've been my best friend, Didi, ever since we were just plebes. You know that I have always defended you and that I will continue to defend you."

I turn to study my friend. Casper William Sewell is a very thin man, who has already started to lose his hair. He is a good sailor, an excellent officer, and a great comrade. He's my only friend, since I'm always too busy to nurture any kind of relationship. Sure, I get along with most people here at the base and there is a certain camaraderie between us. But friendship, true friendship, I can say with certainty that only with Casper.

"Thank you, Casper, you're the best." This time I manage a little smile. Just a small one, but better than none. "I hope at least some of them believe your words."

He looks at me, and then we both turn to see the blue water in front of us. Well, what you actually get to see are the vessels around the dock.

As always, there's a lot of activity. Sailors walking around, in the distance, the noise of helicopter blades, and planes taking off and landing. For years this has been a joint base with the Air Force.

"They weren't just empty words," he says. "Because you keep your distance, some may not wish to acknowledge it, but they know it's true. Bottom line, no one can argue that if they were looking for the best officer for that kind of opportunity, you had to be the first choice, Didi."

Casper is the only person in the world who calls me Didi, and I have no idea where the hell he got the stupid nickname from. I don't love it, which I've told him many times, but today I let it pass. I've had enough confrontation for one day.

We better change the topic.

"What about you?" I ask. "You also have several years of brilliant performance, in addition to vast field experience."

He smiles as he looks down and moves the tip of his shiny black shoe. He's wearing his whites, and I wish I had done the same, the weather is particularly hot today.

"Don't you worry, there'll be something for me," he replies without looking me in the eye. "What are your plans for the weekend? If you want, we can rent a catamaran and go fishing. Maybe it would be fun to invite some friends, but if you prefer, it can be just you and me. It'll be like old times, laughing at the world, and all the crap that surrounds us."

"I have very little to pack, but I want to go to my Hanalei house," I reply, not knowing where that came from, though it's an excellent idea. "I would like to fix something, since I don't know when I'm going to be back."

"You don't have to be alone, Didi."

"I know," I sigh, "and thank you, but I want to enjoy my last days here at my own pace."

I need to disconnect and think about what I'm going to do. San Diego, so close and yet so far from what I want

"You are very different from the other girls I know."

"Well, we've always known that," I answer with a smile on my lips. I've never wanted to be like other girls, I wanted to be my own kind of woman.

Three hours later, dressed in my civilian clothes, I'm boarding a small commercial plane that will take me to the neighboring island of Kauai. That's where I have my house, in front of Wainiha Bay. Well, to call it a house is a big exaggeration. It is just a four hundred square feet cabin, with two rooms and a dining room with an open kitchen.

It is so small, that in order to squeeze in the dining table, I had to tear down one of the walls. In the other room, separated from the living room by wooden blind panels, I put together a queen size bed in which I usually sleep like a baby. Although I have no idea about design, I've tried to make this place my home, spending time painting the walls and looking for the right furniture to bring here.

My father said that it was just a yurt with a beautiful view and the only valuable thing about it was the land. If I'd accepted his help, I could have bought a condominium in one of those bougie complexes that have every luxury you can imagine. However, I was and still am, proud to have been able to buy this little house on my own.

When I get there, the first thing I do is change into my sneakers and go for a run on the beach.

I run along the edge of the water for more than two hours, not caring that my shoes are getting wet, and are becoming increasingly heavy. I need this, to feel the muscles aching in my legs. I let myself be carried away by the wind, going so far I feel I am going to reach the horizon. I arrive home as the sun is staining the sky with pretty colors as if creating a unique masterpiece, the view is so stunning I almost forget the aching of my body. This is good, I embrace the pain, because the wounds of the body heal faster than the sorrows of the soul.

After taking a bath, I drop down on the bed, Morpheus pours some of his sleeping sands and I don't resist his spell.

My phone rings again and then again, I have no idea who would call this early. Yes, for me it is early in the morning, I'm off from work and although the sun already seeps through the thin curtains that cover the windows of my room, I feel a heaviness, like I'm an old woman in the body of an almost thirty one year old.

Whoever is calling can fuck off. Just leave a message, and when I have opened my eyes, I'll get back to you.

Why has this whole matter affected me so much?

Because my credibility as an officer is on the line. I have been dealt a low blow by none other than my own father, certain as I am that he has used his influence.

I feel betrayed, because my father knows how hard I've had to work to get where I am on my own merits. Being a flag officer, he should understand how much reputation means when the lives of those in our care depend largely on our credibility. More than that, I want to be respected, not only as an officer, but also as a person. The military is a world ruled by men, so being a woman isn't always easy.

No matter what anyone thinks, I graduated from the academy with the highest honors, then I earned my masters in naval engineering. My specialty is a secret that I can't discuss openly, let's just say that I work in new technologies, and that's why I've been training with a group of elite sailors. Since I left the academy I have not stopped for a moment. Immediately after graduating, I was first assigned to the Atlantic Surface Force, and then when I asked for a transfer after a year, they sent me to Hawaii, where I have been working ever since.

The phone rings again and when it starts for the fifth time, I decide to take pity on whoever it is and answer.

"Didi! Finally." It's Casper. "Where are you? I was worried, I've been knocking on your door for hours."

"Good morning, Casper," I reply wearily. My friend knows that before drinking my first cup of coffee I'm as friendly as a bear with thorny feet. My day was going perfectly until someone woke me up. Has something happened?

"Didi, are you alright? You never sleep this late."

The clock on my nightstand shows that it's already past nine in the morning.

"There's always a first time," I reply almost rolling my eyes. "It's not *that* late."

For a few seconds neither of us says anything, until Casper breaks the silence.

"Some friends and I decided to go fishing, so if you're still at the base you can come with us."

"I flew to Kauai yesterday, and I'm staying here until Sunday afternoon. So enjoy your trip, Casper, and I hope to see you on the tarmac."

"You know I'll be there," he says and that makes me smile.

After a short farewell, we end the call. I understand Casper's concern, although in a way it overwhelms me. He knows me well, he knows that when I want to be alone, it's because I need my space, to walk at my own pace, with no one around to tell me I should slow down. I have enough of that daily at the base.

So when I leave base, I want to forget the rules and be free.

To be me.

Without ranks, without medals, without thinking of orders.

An hour and a half later, I park my old Jeep in an area east of the island. A few years ago, this was a very popular spot among locals and tourists. Kipu waterfalls, also called the pool of death, after a series of accidents. So the company that owns the land decided to close the access, but I know a way in and I'm an excellent swimmer. My father took care of that at a very young age.

I love coming here, especially as I know I'm not going to find anyone else around. Although the waterfall is small compared to others, it is incredible. My favorite part is a tree on the edge of a ledge, just above the waterhole, where someone had the great idea of hanging some ropes were I can swing like a little monkey before falling in the water.

After finding a safe place to leave my backpack and take off my clothes, I throw myself headlong into the water, swimming to the other side, where in the middle of the tree roots, a thin old metal ladder is anchored to climb up to where the ropes meet.

I climb at full speed, excited for what is coming, check on my bikini and prepare myself to run to gain momentum.

"I hope you're not going to jump," says an unknown voice behind me, almost scaring me to death. "Did you know that this place has restricted access and that this is private property?"

It is the deep, serious, seductive voice of a man.

Feeling safe enough, I smile as I turn to look over my shoulder, although not enough to see my accuser, before answering: "Of course. What, are you going to call the police and report me for trespassing?"

I run and throw myself into the water, with a roar that I hope sounds like a war cry and not the cackling of a chicken.

I land in the water with a huge splash. This is awesome, I love it! I open my eyes beneath the surface to find someone swimming toward me. I surface as fast as I can, I came here to be alone, not to flirt with some stranger, and become a fool's hunting trophy.

I gasp for air, scraping my hair back from my face, ready to make my way to the shore, until he appears in front of me and my intentions are forgotten.

He looks like a gladiator. His bright eyes that seem so dark and intense at the same time. A strong jaw. Wide shoulders, on which thick, black tattoo lines meander and give him an overwhelming attitude of a winner. He moves confidently, comfortable in his own skin. Here is a man who looks at me as if I were his prey. One who makes me want to slide my hands through his short hair and discover what will make those dimples appear.

I'm in trouble.

Big trouble.

"What are you doing here alone?" he asks, looking at me with a frown.

"Well, what do you think? Unless you're a police officer, I don't see why you should care about what I'm doing or not doing."

The Naughty Cop perhaps?

He has a body to die for, not excessively muscular, just to the exact point where he looks incredible.

"What a shame that you're here alone."

"I'm having fun," I answer, not worrying what he thinks. "At least I was before you came here and started playing the cop."

"This is not the place for a pretty girl to come alone, there are a lot of loons everywhere."

He has the nerve to say that.

"Seems I found the only one around these waters."

He laughs, which makes me smile, even if I don't want to. And I wonder, would the crazy one be me for wanting to stay here with him?

Christ, he's a stranger after all.

"That is solvable," he says.

Am I thinking aloud?

"I'm Adrik Houston," he says, pulling his hand out of the water, and offering it to me.

"I'm *Ania,*" I answer, giving him a fake name, and shaking his hand.

In theory he's not a stranger anymore and it seems he won't attack me. However, something tells me that I'm in serious trouble, perhaps the way I have butterflies fluttering in my stomach?

Rule # 3: Slow down and enjoy the pleasure of making her smile.

Chapter THREE

Adrik doesn't take his eyes off me, and to be honest, in the face of his smug demeanor I do the same and stare right back at him.

I refuse to let anyone intimidate me, and this man is not going to be the exception. Whatever direction this is going to go, it will be my choice.

"What is a pretty girl doing in a place like this?"

"Fleeing from idiots who use cheesy pick-up lines," I say, letting out a loud laugh.

"I have some that are even worse, do you want to hear a few? The next is to ask you 'study or work?'"

I laugh again, and even though I just met him two minutes ago, I can say that I like him. A man who has enough balls to laugh at himself is an intelligent man.

I like that.

I can't stand idiots. Frankly, I'm allergic to them.

"Do you want to jump in again?" I ask after a while.

"First off," he replies. "I'm not sure I've got over seeing you jump like a madwoman. I thought I'd have to dive in to rescue you. Haven't you heard how dangerous the pool is?"

Oh no, let's not start with that nonsense, I've had enough of it with my father.

"It's something I've done many times before, and I'm a very good swimmer." It's true, I like to come to this place. I feel as if I was spiritually connected to this place as strange as it sounds. We both look at the crystalline blue pool in front of us. It's magnificent, I could spend hours watching the waterfall without getting bored. That's why I decided to come here.

I needed this. Especially if I'm going to California, and who knows when I'll be able to come back.

God, I'm going to miss this place.

"Are you in your element?" he asks, his attention fixed on me.

His question seems simple, but somehow I think it merits a deeper response.

Why? I don't know.

"I'm a woman of action, I like to be on the move, and if you ask my father, he'll say that I'm like a powder keg. But I have always liked the water, it's an important part of my world."

He stares at me, saying nothing for a few moments, those eyes that I'm still trying to figure out the color of as they seem to darken even more.

"I understand," he says. "You're like the volcanoes that formed these islands. Fire and water, two elements balancing each other out."

Speaking of philosophy...

"Balancing each other out?" I let out a laugh that fills the place as much as the sound of the water falling. "You wouldn't be saying that if you'd seen me angry."

I want to laugh again, but seeing him stops me. Adrik looks serious, his expression is intense, inscrutable, and makes me want to find out what he's thinking.

"I'd like to see it," he declares. "It'd be like a phenomenon of nature. A show worth admiring. Like a storm."

It's my turn to raise my eyebrows and stare at him.

"I think you're reckless," he states. "Like those crazy people on television who hunt hurricanes."

And just like that, we're sharing secrets, hidden beneath lighthearted answers, and quick banter.

"In my line of work I also have to be reckless, when danger is always lurking around the corner."

Don't tell me that he's military too? Relationships with someone from the force aren't prohibited in the code of conduct, but I have enough problems already. And yet, I want to ask him more, I want him to keep talking until I've learned everything there is to know about him. I want to know every little detail about his life, but before any questions can escape from my mouth, I realize that if they do, I will also have to answer any questions he has for me.

And no, I'm not ready to talk about me.

Also, I like the mystery.

Let's keep it interesting.

At least for now.

"So, are you going to jump old man, or has your poor old heart not recovered yet?" I challenge him.

Adrik is nothing like an old man, I'd put him in his late thirties, and very well preserved, by the way, with a body that many college students would kill for. A body that is making my fingers itch to trace the curves of the muscles of his six-pack.

And as for that V that disappears beneath the waistband of his dark blue swim trunks…

"Well, beautiful," he says. "If all you want is to have fun, who am I to deny it?"

He moves away, heading back to the ladder to climb out, as I follow very close behind him.

We jump a couple times more and then take a break to eat a snack, sharing the contents of our respective bags. Adrik brought jerky, almonds, and a couple of tangerines while I have lots of dried fruit and brownies.

He talks a little about being here on the island for almost a week, after a long time without any holidays. "I work long hours every single day, and it's easy to forget about free time and vacations," he explains.

I can relate to this so much.

"We're a pair of workaholics, eh?"

"Workaholic in rehab," he adds smiling. "The doctor prescribed ten days of intensive relaxation."

"How are you managing it?" I ask, mocking concern.

"This is the first conversation I've had in the last six days, since talking with chickens doesn't count."

Oh chickens, there is an abundance of those around the island.

I watch Adrik swimming around, the muscles on his back and arms working hard. He isn't just like a fish in water, Adrik is like Neptune in his element. Dominating the waters.

Dominating me too.

Talking with him feels so easy, and it feels fantastic to let go of the stress for once and just be a normal girl having a good time. I can't help but smile, wishing this would never end.

They say that when you're having fun, time flies, and I've stayed here much longer than I'd planned. But neither of us care, we're having fun, and my worries seem to have stayed behind.

Soon enough I'll have to take care of them. Each day brings its own eagerness. Here and now, I just want to have fun.

"Listen," he says after a while. "It has been very hot since I arrived on the island a few days ago and I'd kill for something cold, so what do you say we go for a shave ice? I know a good place near here, and if you're on your best behavior, I may let you put *li hing mui*."

"For someone who only arrived on the island recently, you speak like a local."

People here usually put a red powder on the ice made from sweet plums. Delicious.

Adrik offers me his hand and I feel that this invitation means much more.

Not allowing myself time to think too hard about hidden secrets in unsaid phrases, I put my hand in his and just go with him.

As we start walking back, the idea of getting a shave ice definitely seems increasingly attractive.

"I'm not getting on that," I say when he points to the black motorcycle parked a few yards from where I left my car. "I thought Prince Charming rode a white horse, and I don't see any of those around."

"I'm no Prince Charming," he replies. "In a fairytale I would be the villain, and this would be my hell horse."

"And suddenly I want to run far, far away from here. The idea of going on your bike doesn't appeal to me at all."

"Don't tell me you're scared," he teases. "We can go as slowly as you like, but I'm sure you'll love feeling the speed, the wind caressing your face, the freedom."

If he only knew…

"No, I wouldn't," I retort. "My Jeep is right there, so you can use your vehicle and I'll use mine. I'm not going to leave my car here, then have to come back to get it, it will put an extra hour on my journey home."

"That is the worst excuse I have ever heard," he scoffs.

"It's not an excuse," I reply. "I'm just being practical."

I quickly locate my keychain inside my bag, it doesn't take long, since apart from the shorts and the t-shirt I was wearing, and a small towel, I don't have much with me. I'm not one of those women who feels the need to carry a lot of stuff, Mary Poppins is not my style.

Practicality above all.

"I'll bring you back to pick up your car. Just come with me," he pleads.

"Follow me," I counter. "Tell me where we're going and then I will lead the way."

It's an invitation but also a challenge.

I dropped the glove, now I hope he dares to pick it up.

Adrik puts on a gray t-shirt and I can't help but think how unfortunate it is that he can't go through life shirtless, since the female population would certainly appreciate the show. He gives me directions to a place I've never been to before, a wooden cabin near Kalapaki beach.

Once we're there, I order the house special, the rainbow, a delicious combination of strawberry, pineapple and blue vanilla, with a large spoonful of condensed milk. Adrik orders the passion fruit one.

Busy with our ices, we walk in comfortable silence along the access road to the beach.

The view is spectacular.

Yes, I'm talking about all that is in front of me. It's not just the sea, nor the beach. It's being here with him. It makes me breathe deeply and at the same time cuts my breath.

Adrik doesn't look like the prince that every girl dreams of. No. He is too masculine for that. He is handsome in a very primitive way, a man who is sure of every step he takes.

We stop at a souvenir store. We enter, discussing all the silly, funny things that surround us. Until a giant rooster made of wood catches my eye.

It's very well made, but who on earth would buy such a preposterous thing to put in their house, or even their office.

It's hilarious.

"Are you thinking of giving me that?" Adrik asks walking over to where I'm looking, making me jump. "I think it's a suitable gift for me."

"Why, because you are a huge chicken?"

He laughs.

"I said it because I have an enormous…"

I open my mouth to speak, while Adrik points to the wooden rooster in front of him.

"Ego, that's for sure," I laugh at him, not with him.

"I can assure you that my ego is up to my abilities and performance. Do you want a test drive?"

Uh huh. Things are starting to get hot around here.

"Ok, Mr. Cocky, tell me then what gift you'd get for me."

"Let's see…"

He walks around the store, until he comes back with a white cup in his hands, which he proudly shows to me.

"A white cup? Seriously? If you're getting bored, you can just go. There's the door, and I've got my own car."

Adrik lets out a laugh as if he finds my comment really funny.

"Calm down, hellion," he chuckles. "This might be a cup, but it's not just any cup."

Holding it out, he turns the cup over so that I can see it's glittery and it has a bright shiny pineapple painted on it.

"A pineapple?" I wrinkle my nose and frown. This is like a hieroglyph that I don't know how to decipher.

"Sure," he replies proudly, looking at me with smiling eyes, small wrinkles forming in the corners, which I find tremendously sexy. An intelligent man with a good sense of humor is very attractive to me and if we add in that he has the body of a centurion, the result is a sex bomb. "You are bright, you stand very proud as if wearing a crown, but you are sweet on the inside."

How the hell do you answer that?

Laughing, of course, because it's the cheesiest but loveliest thing I've heard in a long time.

"Well, you sure are king of the cliché quotes."

We laugh again, as he walks over to pay for the cup, placing it in my hands once it's been gift wrapped.

"Don't even think I'm going to buy that chicken for you," I say after thanking him for the gift.

"Don't worry, I can manage with my big…"

"Ego," I finish his sentence.

"Ok, let's go with my big *ego*," he laughs again. "And the rest too."

We continue walking along the pedestrian promenade, and I'm really enjoying this day. No worries, no pressure, just being me.

"I'd like to take you to dinner this evening, to a place I know. What do you say?"

A smile is drawn on my face, a small triumph that I allow myself. Yes, I like him, it's true. But I also have the same effect on him. He likes me too. I have not lost my touch.

Under the uniform, a woman hides.

A powerful woman.

But then we find it hard to agree on our plans. I insist that we meet at the restaurant, but Adrik insists on picking me up at home.

In the end, I let him win. If he intends to become my stalker, it won't do him much good as I go to the Mainland in two days, so there'll be no one to stalk. Plus he doesn't even know my real name.

One of my favorite things about this island is how quiet it is, here the nightlife is nil, restaurants are usually only open until nine.

"Nothing fancy," I warn him. I did not bring anything fancy to wear, just a couple of summer dresses, although I think I may have something in the closet.

"Nothing fancy," he promises, raising his hands.

We walk to the jeep and I quickly jump in and leave before things can get weird. Like, how was I supposed to say goodbye? A handshake seems too cold and businesslike. A kiss on the cheek is more personal, but doesn't seem appropriate.

At home, I quickly get in the shower, and despite turning on the cold water, my body remains heated, that's the effect this unknown man has on me. I came here looking to rest and relax, now I'm living an adventure with a stranger.

I dry my hair, letting it fall in soft waves down my back. I'm not an expert in makeup, so concealer, mascara, and some lip gloss will have to do the trick. I wear my red dress and flat sandals, the only ones I brought with me. A little perfume here and there and I'm ready.

They say that blondes have more fun, but brunettes also know how to play.

At two minutes before six, there's a knock on the door, and I know for sure who it is.

My pulse accelerates with every step as I walk the very short distance to the entrance of my house.

Adrik.

Undressed he's a god, but even with clothes on he's still a walking temptation. My fingers tingle, my blood burns as he makes me want to unwrap him slowly, like a candy, to discover what's concealed beneath, what his skin tastes like.

Tonight looks like it's going to be very interesting.

He stares at me, almost with his mouth open, saying nothing, until a smile is drawn on his lips.

"You look…" Edible, I can almost hear him finish.

"Another one of your cheesy quotes, Houston?"

"The worst, it's impossible for a man to complete a sentence when he sees a woman like you."

We both laugh, cutting the tension. Sexual tension. We both recognize it and that only increases the flame.

Without wasting any more time, he takes my hand, just letting me grab my handbag and close the door of the house before he leads me to where his black motorcycle is waiting for us.

"This time you have no excuses," he says before putting one of the black helmets in my hands.

The truth is that I appreciate the distraction of riding his bike. In the enclosed space of a car many things can happen and it's too early for that. Yes, yes, I know that I will only be here for the weekend, even so, it's not the right time.

Adrik gets on first, however, he doesn't stop behaving like a gentleman and helps me do the same. As soon as we get on our way, I realize my mistake.

My crass, immense mistake.

Because this is a hell horse indeed. The motorcycle is a giant, vibrating machine, which Adrik drives at full speed and with mastery. At first, my fingers cling timidly to his waist, but five minutes later he takes one of my hands and places it tightly around his chest, not allowing me to remove it, thereby conjuring a spell.

Nor is it lost on me that he's moving between my legs, doing what he knows best. My wicked mind flies faster than the vehicle we are going on and I'm glad, I'm *really* glad that he can't read my mind.

"I hope I don't look like a complete mess now," I grumble as I take off my helmet when we arrive.

It took me so long to tame my hair, now goodbye to the loose waves, and hello to the bird's nest.

"You always look beautiful," he replies, giving me a quick, dry kiss on the lips, which takes me by surprise, especially when I find I want more.

Much more.

"You've known me for less than twelve hours and you're already saying things like that?" I tease. "You are definitely the master of cliché."

I walk in front of Adrik, and he guides me with one hand on the lower part of my back. The contact of his skin through the thin cotton fabric of my dress burns me.

My body is on DEFCON 1.

It's Saturday, so the place is quite crowded, but to our luck we're informed that in a few minutes they'll have a table for two on the terrace that overlooks the sea, so for now we settle in the wicker chairs and order our drinks.

"Do you come here often?" I ask while we look at the menus.

"Your turn for a cheesy quote, Ania?" he mocks and we both laugh at the absurd comment. "Actually, it's the second time I've been here," he says, once we've been seated at our table, where a gentle sea breeze ruffles my hair. I raise my eyebrows inviting him to continue. "A colleague from… from my job got married here last summer, and we were all invited."

The waitress returns to take our orders, and everything looks so delicious that we ask for several dishes to share.

"Look, the sun is setting!" I practically yell out like a young girl, but it really is very beautiful, making tonight seem extra special.

Adrik appears so relaxed, a man at ease in his sun-kissed skin. With every smile I wonder what it'd be like being with him on a normal day. Having dinner in my apartment and laughing at small things, with his bad jokes and cheesy quotes.

But I'm not a fool and I know better. Love at first sight doesn't exist, it only happens in Hallmark movies, and I'm not acting out a scripted role here.

We have dinner talking about everything and nothing. Neither of us specifically mentions what they do, which is a relief. As a rule, men react in one of two ways when they learn that I'm a naval officer. The first is that they begin asking all kinds of stupid questions about war. War is terrible, period. Although I love my work, I take no pleasure in remembering the consequences. The second is that they run away in terror, as if a woman with pants tightly tied at the waist is a mythological creature to be feared, even though a pair of bands on my shoulders doesn't make me Medusa.

After more than three drinks of a thing called Kauaiian Punch, a tasty mixture of pineapple and orange juice, black berry syrup, coconut puree, and rum, my head starts to feel dizzy.

Adrik doesn't drink more than mineral water, which I appreciate, as he's driving his giant vibrator. Sorry, his bike. Damn alcohol makes me silly.

Damn hormones block my defenses.

Damn the heat.

At about fifteen minutes to nine our waitress comes to announce that we must pay the bill, because the restaurant is about to close.

"Don't even think about it," he insists when I get out some cash from my wallet. "My grandfather taught me well. I would never let a woman I invited to dinner pay her share."

"How old fashioned, Mr. Houston."

He gives a crooked grin.

"In some ways, but in other ways I'm very progressive."

"Like?"

"You'll have to find that out for yourself."

Challenge accepted.

We leave the restaurant, as he lets me walk in front, I look over my shoulder while coquettishly swinging my hips. The hand on my back travels to my hip, tightening its grip, as his breath caresses my neck, his hand continues down my torso, going down, down, until it reaches my bare thighs.

Taking advantage of the darkness of the parking lot, his curious fingers expertly slide under the hem of my dress and climb up to where he finds me wet and warm.

I growl in frustration as I realize that I'm ready for a man like this, someone who excites me and doesn't waste time messing around.

"Come with me, Ania," he pleads, breaking off his teasing touch. "Come with me to my hotel."

"No," I sigh as I shake my head, determined to resist.

"Don't say no, I know you want this as much as I do."

Yes, it is true, of course it is true.

"Time is running out, just give me tonight."

I want to say yes, I really do. However, I play the best card in my deck.

"If fate wants us to be together, we will meet again."

Such is his confusion that he loosens his grip on my waist, allowing me enough space to escape.

I walk toward the street, looking for the nearest taxi.

If fate wants... strong words.

Now I'm dying to know what it is that we have.

Rule # 4: Anticipation is an underrated pleasure. It's not just about the destination, but also enjoying the trip.

Chapter FOUR

When I get home, my skin is still tingling, the imprint of his mouth remains on my neck, and something deep inside tells me that it will be like that for a while.

Everything has become unbalanced and that has made me run. I don't like that the prevailing order that I always strive so hard for, feels threatened.

The rational part of my brain wonders if it's because I lack anyone to compare Adrik to. My dry spell has lasted for what seems like forever.

What did I expect? I live in a men's world. Competitive men, to be exact, who would expect me to give up my dreams for them. They'd put a thousand obstacles and impediments in my way to stop me from pursuing my career. So here I stand, waging war with no allies. Something I've learned is to never sleep with your colleagues if you want to be taken seriously, no matter how tempted you may be. Over the years, I've heard many unpleasant rumors and, frankly, I prefer being called the Arctic Empress over providing more gossip for the entire base. After my many years in the force I can confidently say that men are the greatest gossips in the world.

My room is as I left it, nothing has changed. The same walls, the same comforter on the bed, my iPad remains on the bedside table. Everything is the same yet different, alien, as this was someone else's room.

I take the brush and begin to untangle the dark strands of my hair with care—or perhaps not so much care—hopefully my thoughts will untangle at the same time as I manage to tame the knots.

My body feels upset and anxious after Adrik's hands left me excited, wanting more.

Burning on a slow flame.

But I can't succumb and I won't.

Once again I let my brain win the fight and let the hormones resent it, the flesh cries out, the desire is still there, burning like a volcano, ready to erupt, and take everything in its path.

If only…

This situation overwhelms me, and I need to return to my world to regain control. I need to be *me* again.

Lieutenant Jordania Zanetti, taking the reins, the woman who is used to having the pan by the handle.

Yes. Take back control.

Excellent idea.

I'll take the morning flight back to Honolulu. I need to head back a.s.a.p. as I have a lot to do, packing up all my things as I prepare for my new life at the NBSD.

I make a reservation on the first flight, which leaves at six o'clock in the morning from Kauai airport. Hopefully before the clock strikes seven, I'll be at Pearl Harbor-Hickam.

I'm not running away. Of course not, I'm offended at the mere suggestion.

I'm just going back to the base with a cool head, ready to pack my stuff and leave for the Mainland. I'm a responsible person after all.

After the takeoff, I look out at the dark ocean as we fly over, and once I approach the base I feel more like myself again. The madness I felt seems to have left my body, and in return I have regained the force that has always kept me whole.

Control.

I think some would say that it is sanity, but I would call it quintessence, the ether, the fifth element.

Not allowing myself the luxury of thinking too much, I mechanically start packing my things. Luckily, unlike some of the other officers, I never bothered acquiring any large appliances, I just have the basics. Five boxes and four suitcases later, everything is packed and ready to be transported to the airport, the boxes taped up as I say goodbye to my life in Hawaii. This life is so volatile, one day you're here, tomorrow you could be reporting on the other side of the world.

Despite the fatigue, I don't sleep much, and before I know it it's five in the morning I'm ready to go, dressed in my daily service uniform, my hair in a low bun, impeccable as always.

If I say I'm surprised to find my father waiting outside, I would be lying.

"Good morning, Admiral," I greet him formally as my superior, raising my right hand.

"Hey, kid," he answers, stopping me as he takes me by the arm. "I've made arrangements for your arrival, so you don't have to worry about anything."

"Thank you, Dad," I say, unable to look him in the eye.

My father's entire body is tense, and I want to believe that's because of the way our last conversation ended.

"You are my only daughter, Jordania," he adds quietly and firmly, without letting go of my elbow. "All I want is your happiness, despite what you may be thinking right now."

His words feel like a wrecking ball hitting me in the abdomen, leaving me breathless, and preventing the words that are stuck in my throat to leave my mouth.

"Thank you," I manage to answer at last.

In a gesture which takes me totally by surprise, my father hugs me. This is not normal, much less in front of so many people, because despite the early hour, there are at least thirty on the tarmac.

"I've always been proud of you," he whispers after hugging me.

I let him hold me briefly because I really need a moment as a couple of tears have escaped and I want to dry them before anyone notices.

I don't like to show my emotions, and sometimes I need to submerge my feelings, acting in self-defense, of course.

Distracted by my father's farewell, I climb the stairs and look for my place, then a face I didn't expect to see greets me, drawing a smile from ear to ear.

"Lieutenant Zanetti."

My mouth opens a couple of times, before I can respond.

"Casper, what are you doing here?"

"Surprise," he replies, still smiling.

"Are you going to the mainland too?"

"An opportunity opened, Lieutenant. I knew several days ago that I was heading to the amphibious base in Coronado, I was just waiting for a good moment to tell you, then they told you about your transfer, so here I am. We will be close, not in the same place, but at least in the same city."

Not in the same place, I have to remind myself. I care for Casper, but he's like a mother hen.

"Well, this has certainly been a surprise," I admit.

"A good or bad one?"

"Good, of course." I force a smile. My trip to California couldn't be starting in a better way, but why do I feel as if I were lying? "Besides, it's not like we're going to train for SEALs, I'm not going to become GI Jane. So you won't see me at the base barbershop, shaving my head like Britney."

"Glad to hear it, that reassures me. Anyway, I have so many ideas and plans for us. I'm going to rent an apartment in the city, close to the beach, we could stay there when we get time off. There's so much to see and do in San Diego."

Casper chatters non-stop throughout the flight and by the time we finally land more than five hours later, my head is about to explode and it's not due to the turbulent flight.

"Lieutenant Zanetti, I hope you had a good flight," greets a dark-haired sailor as he approaches me. "I'm Chief Hernandez. Admiral Zanetti commissioned me to take you to your accommodation. If you'd be so kind as to follow me, it's a short drive to Pacific Beacon."

Casper looks at me in surprise, but I choose not to give further explanation, just shrugging as I follow my guide.

"Your luggage is being taken care of," he informs me as we leave for the parking lot.

The drive isn't actually that short but at least it's scenic, and the weather here is amazing. Eventually we arrive at a building that could pass for a modern, new hotel. I'm aware they've only recently built this accommodation, and that a good amount of money was invested. First impression is that it was a wise decision as the previous barracks were outdated.

"There you go, ma'am," says Hernandez. "I printed a map to help you locate the facilities and amenities. There are similar buildings and the complex is big, it's easy to get lost until you've familiarized yourself. The base is just a short walk away, but please call if you wish me to organize a ride for you."

"A walk is fine with me, thank you, Hernandez."

After carrying my belongings to my new dwelling, I thank the man, and then start exploring the place.

The apartment is beautiful, I have to say, and I feel a bit spoiled. I read in the newspaper a couple years ago how the Navy had said goodbye to the barracks and invested in these buildings for single sailors, but they are nicer than what I imagined.

It's an open plan, the kitchen separated from the living room by a breakfast bar. In the back, a door leads to a bedroom with a queen size bed with a plastic-lined mattress, a huge television on the dresser, and two bedside tables, that I guess were brought here by my father's orders. The bathroom is big and there is a walk in closet too. What I like most are the large windows and the small balcony, which let in plenty of light along with a gentle breeze.

There is no time to waste, but at least I don't have to do any cleaning. Three hours later, I've unpacked most of my things and I'm hanging the last of my belongings in the closet, plus the paper bag with the pineapple mug, a memento of what could have been but wasn't meant to be.

There's a knock on the door and I'm almost certain it'll be Casper, who won't have taken more than half an hour to find me.

"Lieutenant Zanetti," says a sailor waiting in the doorway. "This is for you."

He gives me a sealed envelope, marked with my name, then takes his leave.

The orders that I must follow. Tomorrow morning I will start the training and all it entails.

I'm excited, but also very restless. I must admit that I'm terrified of the unknown, but at the same time ready for the new challenge.

I search the base map for the supermarket and hurry to do some shopping. The fridge is empty and the idea of going to the dining facilities sounds very unappealing.

Casper has already called at least half a dozen times, insisting that we should go out and familiarize ourselves with the city, and find new favorite spots to hang out, but I'm tired and don't feel like seeing anyone. Right now, all I feel like doing is lying in my new bed, wishing that he—Adrik Houston—were here with me, finishing off what he started in Kauai, with those talented fingers of his between my legs.

Tuesday.

Seven in the morning.

I stand in front of the full-length mirror as I slip on the silk camisole that I usually wear under my uniform. I like pretty underwear, lace, silks, fancy prints. I might be a navy junior officer, but I'm still a woman and there's no reason I can't keep my true essence concealed under my uniform, like a little secret that only I know.

In the memorandum I received, we were ordered to attend in our daily service uniform, so I chose the khaki, which is much more practical than the white one which, by the way, gets stained so easily, and everyone secretly hates it.

I watch my reflection in the mirror in front of me, today I've decided to wear my mother's pearl studs, my father bought them with his first salary and it was her favorite piece of jewelry she ever owned, well, that's one of the few stories he has told me about her. *Help me, mother*, I'm ready to tackle this task, in a few months I'm going to say mission accomplished and ask my command for a transfer to the Warfare Command.

I believe I can, so I will.

Picking up my leather briefcase with everything I need for the day along with an extra-large cup of coffee, I go to the D4 building, where I will be carrying out my training.

I got this, I wasn't born to be average. Just a reminder, after finishing with this, no one will say it was just because I'm a Zanetti.

Upon entering the room, I meet a couple of officers, who like me, have decided to arrive early, and I'm not surprised to see they're a little older than me. Anderson and Thomson appear to be good guys, and although we're not here to make friends, at least at first glance there's no antipathy.

I vaguely remember Thomson from the academy, I think he was about to graduate when I was in my plebe year, while Anderson was transferred to the OCS directly from the Georgetown faculty of political science.

"Weren't you married to Sanders?" Thomson asks me. "How is he? I haven't seen him in years."

"We never made it to the altar, so I have no idea. I haven't seen him in a long time either."

The man's face blushes, clearly embarrassed by his blunder.

"No worries, Lieutenant," I add, trying to lighten the atmosphere, not wanting to delve into that very unpleasant part of my past. Better it happened before the wedding than after. I was neither the first nor will I be the last to break off an engagement.

Fortunately, Anderson changes the conversation to a much lighter topic. Once we start talking about our experiences in the fleet and the tours we've participated in, I'm in my element.

In less than ten minutes our instructor arrives and the empty chairs begin to fill up.

We are twelve in total, ten men and two women. The other female officer is a short-haired blonde girl, who is accompanied by two other male officers and, after greeting everyone, sits on the other side of the long boardroom table.

"Good morning, officers," greets our instructor when he enters the room, as we all stand to greet him properly. "I'm Captain Nolan."

The captain begins to explain the object of our training. The information must be treated with great discretion, but in a nutshell, we will learn what is necessary in order to command a destroyer, a frigate or a small submarine, none of which I love, but I understand is necessary training in order to rise in the ranks. As sailors we must be prepared. Always.

After more than five hours of class, we finish the session, then head out to grab a light lunch, because this afternoon we expect an equally intense dose.

The rest of the week follows more or less the same routine, with the first few days mostly theoretical. Do you remember those college classes where you had to consume all the books and then know what you were supposed to do? Well, this is more or less the same, only in practice there are endless possibilities that can send everything to shit, and as the officers in charge that is what we have to avoid.

The days fly by, and I barely have time to get out on my bike for some exercise. All of our brains are fried after our first test. We all agreed to go together to the dining facilities to celebrate the fact that we survived our first week, although barely.

I have made some friends. Grace Carr, the other officer with whom I'm leading the training is nice, but quiet, so I usually find myself carrying the weight of the conversation with the rest of the group.

"What are your plans for this afternoon?" Kevin Levitt, one of my classmates, asks me.

"I might go and look for a car. I'm thinking if I want to leave the base, it'd be best to buy something."

"Do you have something in mind?"

"A hybrid would be great," I admit. "Although knowing me, I'll probably end up buying a Jeep."

Of course, cars, the favorite topic of men, so they immediately begin to give me advice, opinions, and so on. Without paying much attention, I say goodbye to everyone, ready to return to my house to change my clothes. I have a lot to catch up on, the academic burden is overwhelming, so it takes up most of the time.

As I walk back, my phone rings. It's Casper, and when I tell him of my plans, he insists I won't need a car as he'll happily take me wherever I need to go.

He is my friend and I care about him, but I find it overwhelming that he wants to go with me everywhere, like we're Siamese twins. Independence is my middle name, that's how I was raised and I have no wish to change.

"You know what, Didi?" he says, changing the subject. "Your name is on everyone's tongue at the base, all the guys are talking about you. You've made a great impression, rumors are already circulating about the amazing and beautiful daughter of Admiral Zanetti."

"Don't fuck with me! Why would everyone be talking about me when I only just got here?" I protest.

It's been only a few days after all.

"This is a small world, you know that," he replies. "And as your best friend, I've told them all that you're the best officer I know, always totally professional, focused and hardworking, so if they want something with you, if they think they have a chance, they are wasting their time."

Damn it, here we go again.

Gossip!

I thank Casper, but end the conversation with a bad taste in my mouth. However, nothing prepares me for what comes next.

I walk along the narrow footbridge, heading to the lodging hall. I'm fuming, so the cool breeze is welcome. Maybe it'll help calm me down, because in this mood I wouldn't buy a car but a war tank.

"It seems that destiny is determined to bring us together," a deep male voice whispers in my ear.

I turn around, surprised to see *him* there, a smirking male vision dressed in a uniform like mine.

"Good afternoon, Lieutenant Zanetti," he says, reading the badge hanging from my uniform.

I take in the bars on his shoulders, the embroidery on his hat, and I feel dizzy as my head twirls.

I swear the floor shakes.

Earthquake!

"Commander..." I manage to say when the air returns to my lungs.

"What a surprise," he adds mockingly. "Right?"

Can you tell?

I was definitely not ready for this.

Rule # 5: Don't overwhelm her, wait for the right moment and then, only then, be implacable.

Chapter FIVE

"So, Lieutenant, aren't you glad to see me?"

The bastard has the nerve to smile, a smile that would melt my panties any other time.

But not now, *of course*.

"Commander..." I repeat like an idiot, it being the only word I can articulate.

"It seems I have left you speechless," he laughs. "If you want we can walk together for a while. I'm heading to the lodging halls."

I frown, dark black clouds loom overhead. Shit. This is a fucking mess.

"Why would I want to?" I finally manage a coherent sentence. "I'm perfectly fine walking by myself."

Thank God.

"Destiny, remember?" He reminds me of my words from our brief encounter in Kauai. "Don't make that face, *Ania,* it was you who put the challenge."

Yes, it was me, because at that moment I thought I would never see him again. Fuck, in such a big world, why the hell did we have to end up on the same base?

Besides, he is my superior. A *Commander,* for fuck's sake.

"That was stupid of me," I glare.

Yes, it was a mistake, a stupid mistake.

"And yet, destiny insists on throwing us together."

He keeps smiling and my lady bits start tingling.

Don't go wild, hormones, I'll keep you happy watching Magic Mike later tonight.

"Well, Commander Houston…" I start, but he cuts me off.

"Why do you address me that way?" he asks, staring into my eyes. "When we were in Kauai you called me Adrik, and I really like hearing my name come from your lips."

"Back then I didn't know you were my superior. If I had known…"

He stares, eyes shadowed by his hat.

"If you had known, what?"

He deserves my challenging attitude.

"Things would not have gone so far between us. If I had been aware of who you are …"

Never, never, would I have allowed myself to be carried away by desire.

"I'm a single man, so what's the problem? Are you married?"

"Of course not! How could you even think that?" I answer indignantly. I would never have allowed him to lay a hand on me if I'd been in a committed relationship with another person.

At that moment someone runs by. It's Anderson in his running gear and he gives us a brief salute.

"Sir, ma'am," he says, running by where we're standing.

Adrik, sorry, Commander Houston, frowns at me.

"You're Jordania Zanetti," he states. "I heard my officers talking about the remarkable Lieutenant Zanetti, but frankly, I had no idea it was you, the golden girl of the Navy."

My reputation precedes me. *Great.*

"Yes, sir. It's true, I *am* Jordania Zanetti." I use the formal tone on purpose, it's time to set some boundaries. "But I pay no attention to base gossip, I'm just here to serve, same as any other sailor."

"Of course you are," he says. "That's a beautiful name, by the way. It suits you."

"Thank you, but that's irrelevant." I rebuke him and he raises his eyebrows in response. "Rumors spread faster than wildfire here at the base and since I've never liked being the subject of gossip, I won't be adding fuel to the fire by going out with you."

We're standing on the footbridge, which is the only way for people to come from the base to the lodging halls.

The schoolyard 2.0.

"At least now I get why everyone has been talking about you," he replies, a mocking smile on his lips. "And I haven't actually asked you out. Yet."

Damn cocky man.

Why does he have to look so good in his uniform?

I want to run off with him to my condo and eat him up with a tiny spoon.

"Well then," I say, as the color rises in my face as I think about all the dirty things I'd like to do with him. "We're all good. It has been a pleasure to speak with you, Commander. Now if you'll excuse me, I have things to do."

I take my leave, being as polite as formal protocol demands, but he takes me by the arm and murmurs in my ear, making me shiver.

"Run if you must, Jordania." My name sounds like a challenge on his lips. "But it'll only make things more interesting."

This infuriating man has had the last word and I don't like it one bit.

Control, Jordan, I have to remind myself with every step I take toward my accommodation.

Control, what a good impression I give. If only it were true.

Being busy is a blessing. The first task I have to accomplish is buying a new car. I don't have my old Jeep here and this city wasn't made for public transport. At least that's what I've heard around the base.

I have some idea of what I want, so several hours later, after haggling with a rather insistent seller, it's starting to get dark as I turn into the street leading to the base driving my brand new car. It's not the hybrid that I planned to buy, but I still think I made a great choice since I didn't leave the dealership with a red convertible.

I smile, looking around, enjoying the new car smell. It's the latest generation so it's really comfortable, plus it has all the advantages of an all-terrain vehicle.

The best of both worlds.

Arriving at the covered parking lot, I collect my things, then activate the alarm, feeling pretty pleased with myself as I enter the building where my new home is located. It may only be temporary, but it's home, after all. I can't help being in a good mood, proud with the result of my excursion, until the sight of a certain male figure, wrapped in worn jeans, boots, and a dark T-shirt, stops me.

Adrik is sitting in one of the huge patio chairs with his phone in one hand. He just has to be on my path.

He stands and parks his body beside the glass door.

"Wow," he says, realizing that I'm approaching, looking at the chunky watch on his left wrist. "It took you a long time to get home."

I lift my chin before answering.

"If I'd known you were here waiting for me, I would've taken even longer." My reply is scathing; he's not in uniform, and neither am I, so I can answer him however I want.

"Let's go to dinner. I'm hungry."

Who the fuck does he think he is? I'm not a newly enlisted sailor who'll jump to obey his orders.

I take a couple more steps toward the threshold of the building. I need a door with several locks in between us.

"Bon appétit," I answer. "I have better things to do."

Not really, but that is something he does not need to know, it would only give him more ammunition against me.

"Don't tease me, Jordania," he warns, approaching me.

I manage to dodge him while I look for the keys to open the door to enable me to flee to the little security the building has to offer.

"That is precisely what I'm trying to avoid, Commander. Good night."

I close the heavy glass door behind me in a rather theatrical gesture, and don't risk waiting for the elevator to arrive, instead using the stairs, but to my misfortune my apartment is on the sixth floor, and there are many sections to climb. At least it counts as cardio, like sex, without the fun. The aching of my legs reminds me that I need to locate the facility's gym.

"Stop following me," I yell when I notice he's right behind me.

My legs are long, but he's faster than me.

"As it happens, I live here too," he replies smirking.

"Why? You're a senior officer, you should be in another building far away from here."

"The joys of military life. Turns out there's no other accommodation available for me at the moment."

No way…

I'm fucked.

"Then go to your own accommodation. Or go have dinner—didn't you say you were hungry?"

"Indeed," he acknowledges, looking at me intensely, I'm afraid he's hungry but not for food. "I still am."

"Luckily for you there is a Subway shop in the lobby."

The way he looks at me turns my world upside down.

Is he going to kiss me?

Two words jump in my head: Yes, please!

But I was wrong. This is not a kiss, it's a full-force attack. One that, I must admit, I crave shamelessly. My defenses crumble before him, as his hands grab my waist to pull me against the hardness of his body, trapping me against the wall.

I'm a moth drawn by the spell of the flame, unable to resist. A part of me, the part that knows the destructive power of fire, urges me to move away, to protect myself. But I'm succumbing, all I can do is squeeze his shoulders as I sink my short nails into his hard muscles, loving his grunt as his tongue mingles with mine, delighting in my taste.

The red hot heat of our bodies sparks and crackles where they touch. I want the nuisance of our clothes to disappear, so I can feel his skin caressing mine.

His hand slides down my neck, followed by his lips, looking for the low neckline of my cotton top.

"No, Adrik…" I protest weakly, as my legs struggle to hold me up. "We shouldn't."

He groans before lifting his gaze to meet mine. His dark grey eyes look smoky in the dim light of the stairs.

"Have dinner with me, Jordania," he insists. "Or better still, come up to my apartment. It's on the top floor and the view is amazing. We can order take-out."

His words break the spell.

I'm not anyone's inflatable doll.

I'm not a hot body to fuck and leave.

"No. I'm not coming to your apartment. We're not doing this."

He looks at me with an inscrutable expression, while his eyes focus on my still heavy chest.

"Why do you insist on denying what's between us?"

"There is nothing between us," I answer. "Nor will there ever be."

"You want me and you know it full well," he states arrogantly.

Wanting him isn't the problem. It's dealing with the consequences afterwards. No, thank you.

"I don't!" I insist.

Adrik raises his eyebrows. "So you do what we've been doing with anyone who happens to approach you?"

Fucking smug bastard makes me want to smash his perfect white teeth with my bare fist.

"Of course not! Don't be so insulting, I'm not a slut."

He keeps staring at me, his jaw so tight that I think his teeth might break at any moment.

"I beg your pardon, ma'am, I didn't mean to insult you," he replies after a few seconds of tense silence. "I was just making a point. I don't understand, what are you afraid of, Jordania?"

"I'm not afraid of anything."

"A ship in harbor is safe, Jordania, but that's not why ships are built."

I roll my eyes in such dramatic fashion… if he is trying to seduce me shooting cheesy pick-up lines, he's wasting his time.

"Then come to dinner with me," he repeats stubbornly.

I sigh, my will is about to falter.

Nevertheless…

"I'm sorry, I have homework for tomorrow, I just started instruction, and I have to make sure I do everything well. I don't want to mess up and only pass because of who my father is."

A smile is drawn on his lips, he seems happy with my answer.

"Well, beautiful. You're in luck, I passed this training with flying colors." Of course he did. "So I can help you, if you let me."

Why does he have to be so insistent? The worst part is that my resolve is weakening.

"Just go and have dinner, you said you were hungry."

Any argument is good as long as he leaves me alone.

"How about I go for Chinese food while you get ready? Give me your apartment number and see you there in half an hour," he counters.

Insistent.

Persistent.

Even more stubborn than me.

Why does he have to be so attractive?

This is doomed to fail and it hasn't even begun.

But then the blurry image of a meek, calm, malleable little man comes to my mind. What would I do with such a man? I'd be bored out of my brains within five minutes, without a doubt.

I think about saying no, but I really want to accept for the sake of my classes, *of course*.

How problematic can it be? No one needs to find out, and if he lives in the same building. And if I'm honest, a little help wouldn't hurt. I have to get some staff accounts, sort some operating expenses, maybe not for tomorrow, but there is no denying that some help would be nice.

"Kung Pao Chicken?" he asks, knowing I'm about to say yes, having hesitated for several minutes.

"Okay, but hold the peanuts. I'm allergic."

"Really? Kung Pao without nuts? You're certainly one of a kind, Jordania Zanetti."

Just as well, I might add. The world is not prepared for more than one of me.

"And bring spring rolls, I live in six twenty."

Leaving him standing there savoring his triumph, I climb the remaining section of the stairs and go to my condo.

This is going to be an interesting night, without doubt.

Will I be able to deal with the consequences?

I'd better be.

For my own good I must be.

Rule # 6: If you want to capture a women's heart, then pay attention to the details.

Chapter SIX

I have to lower my temperature, I need something to switch off, or at least abate, this heat that consumes me, and won't let me breathe.

The first thing that comes to mind is a cold shower, so I run to the bathroom, leaving a trail of clothes behind me. As soon as the water touches my heated skin, the memories return. Our first encounter in the waterfall, the intensity of his gaze, the sensation of his hands touching me everywhere. I feel like an idiot, a fool who cannot resist the urgency, the desire.

Adrik is the kind of man who could kill me. He could really hurt me, cause a lot of damage, and I'm not just talking about physically.

I have to be cautious, keep my feet on the ground, although I have no idea how. It was so much easier when I was able to keep my defenses high to prevent anyone from getting too close.

What the hell is wrong with me?

Why can't I resist?

I have to consider this as just another trial, a new challenge, I decide while I soap up. That's all it is, and I'll deal with it the same way as I cope with being a female officer in charge of a squad of sailors loaded with testosterone. This is really no different, is it?

I've dealt with that and I'll deal with this.

Yes, ladies and gentlemen, Adrik Houston will soon be just another test that I've passed.

My name is on the line of fire.

I'm afraid in the most literal sense.

I'm searching through my drawers for my most demure garment, and about to put on my granny underwear, when I hear someone knocking on the door, so I grab the first thing that I find, which is some jeans and an academy sweatshirt.

The windows are wide open and a soft breeze is coming from the bay, my hair is still wet and loose, I'm not wearing a lick of makeup or perfume, although I have put some of my favorite body lotion on.

As I walk through the living room of my apartment I stop when I realize there are only a couple of tall stools at the breakfast bar.

Where are we supposed to sit for dinner?

There's another loud knock on the door—it seems that patience isn't one of Commander Houston's strengths. I open the door to find him standing there, balancing two paper bags, and a glass bottle containing amber liquid. Iced tea, I assume.

"Houston, we have a problem," I say as he walks in and puts the packages on the kitchen counter.

"The only problem we have is that you don't want to give me what I want," he says, leaning toward me, tempting me to give in.

Nuh uh, commander. You came here to help me, not to heat up my hormones.

And you don't play fair.

It is hard to ignore his words, because it's something I don't want to do but I know that I can't let desire be the captain of this ship.

Jesus, take the wheel.

"The problem is that my house is empty, so I don't have a table and chairs where we can sit to have dinner." Fortunately, for now his attention is focused on the apartment and not on me.

"We can always use your bed," he suggests with a mischievous gleam in his smoky eyes.

If my stomach wasn't making all kinds of sounds because I'm ravenously hungry, I'd send him to hell, or at least out into the corridor.

"Sorry, Commander, but my bed is off-limits so you need to think again."

"Are you afraid of me, Jordania?" He's close, maybe too close.

"No," I insist. "I just hate food crumbs between the sheets."

I don't know where I got that one from, but it's a pretty great excuse.

"Then we'll have to settle for these stools or the floor."

"The stools are definitely a better option," I reply, glancing down at the clean but undoubtedly cold floor tiles. "What do you have in there?"

Adrik starts unloading the boxes and then places a big pineapple on the counter.

"A pineapple?" *What the heck?*

He shrugs. "What can I say? I have a weakness for sweet girls with thick skin."

"Thank God, I'm not that sweet."

He chuckles before opening the first food box.

After a quick dinner, flirting is replaced by piles of paper and meticulous notes. It turns out that Adrik is an excellent teacher, patient and dedicated. Those little award ribbons hanging from his uniform didn't come from a cereal box, from what I remember I think he had a Purple Heart ribbon and a Legion of Merit. The reason becomes clearer with every passing minute, as we highlight many points and make a thousand notes in my yellow legal pad.

"What's first thing in a destroyer's job description?" he asks me.

"Be the bodyguards of the flag ship." This is something we learned in basic training. "Defend the carrier against enemies attack."

"Good, now a destroyer like the Benfold has more than two hundred recruits, plus the commissioned officers, and the chief petty officers, which adds up to almost three hundred people on board," he explains, leafing through the papers in his hand, marking again the important points. "For supplies, you must take into account the number of people you have on board, how many days the mission will last, plus the ports where you'll make stops as is crucial that you don't run out of food. The crew in charge keeps the ship afloat, and comfort is the first thing you should keep in mind. Food and fuel are your two top priorities, so you have to be prepared for any emergencies that may arise. The size of the vessel does not matter, we lived in a world where the risk of war is always present so you need to be prepared."

"Fuel and food." Easier said than done.

There are so many variables and it is a lot to consider. Our staff is more than formulas and numbers on paper.

"Trust the crew and their skills. Delegate everything you can or you will go crazy. Remember that even the best captain has its limits and you will have to accept help from your subordinates. Make your mark from day one, impose your seal, Jordania, and don't let yourself be overwhelmed."

Thinking about it, my knees tremble, this is a great responsibility. But I have to be able to cope with it.

This is not my first rodeo, I have been forged by the sea. My bones are made of titanium.

"I haven't even reached that point yet and I'm already overwhelmed. It's too much."

"I'm sure you're up for the challenge. That's what this course is all about, ensuring that you are ready to face the challenge competently."

"You seem to have more confidence in me than I do."

Adrik ignores my comment and we return to the spreadsheet that is open on my laptop.

Between the papers there are open food boxes, we ate straight from them as I couldn't bother getting plates.

The destroyer we are talking about is a ship of the Arleigh Burke class, all of those are structurally similar, marvels of steel built with stealth technology that is more than five hundred feet long and sixty six feet wide plus a draught of thirty three feet, that makes them extremely stable even in heavy seas, which, at its maximum capacity, weighs more than nine thousand tons. In addition, it is equipped to launch missiles and anti-aircraft attack weaponry, as well as anti-submarine weaponry.

It is an engineering wonder, the engine is powerful and gives the vessel great speed and agility. This is what I like, learning everything about what we currently have and seeing how we can improve it. The innovations, all the advances, everything that helps keep our staff and country safe.

It is fascinating.

"Will you participate in the RIMPAC?" he asks after a while.

This is the world's largest international naval exercise and the main objective is to put into practice everything we learn in training, Marines, Air Force and Navy participate. Many ships of the fleet participate as well as more than twenty other countries, the atmosphere is loaded with emotion—and exhaustion—the maneuvers are intense and prepare us for anti-submarine attacks, tactical air defense operations, and strategic naval warfare against marine and inland targets. Everyone competes to be the best.

"I have no idea. Back in Hawaii, I was training with my squad for it, but isn't it too soon for that here?"

"I haven't heard anything about it yet," he admits. "Because I haven't been here for almost two years. Hopefully I can stay here permanently but you never know, they haven't relocated me yet."

"What is your plan?" I ask, genuinely interested.

I put down the papers and focus my attention on him.

"To stay here in mainland. The years are passing by and I'm not getting any younger." He smiles, looking around the kitchen, but not focusing on any specific place. "My grandparents moved some years ago to a house here in East County. They did it to be closer to me, but I still don't get to see them as much as I would like, which is a shame, because they are the only thing I have left."

He smiles sadly, and I suddenly have the urge to hug him, but instead I hold on to the pencil in my hand, as if it were a lifeline.

We are being friends now, rather than student and teacher.

"Wow," I sigh. My father is all the family I have left, but I've no idea if he has ever thought about staying in one place just to spend time with me. I've very few memories of him being just 'my dad'. Some are from our nights in the Cape Cod house, listening to Van Morrison while he sang "Brown Eyed Girl" to me.

Do you remember when we used to sing…

Sha la la la la la la la la la la te da

My heart shrivels a little when I wonder what it would have been like if my mother were still alive.

I've never had a close relationship with another woman, a mother figure. The nannies my father hired to look after me while I was growing up did their job, but the emptiness was still there. It was never the same.

Is it possible to miss someone I never met?

"I'm not a spring chicken anymore, *living la vida loca* was never my thing. I've decided maybe it's time to settle somewhere more permanent, put down some roots," he says, glancing over at the closed door of the balcony. "So I just bought a house here in San Diego, in East Village, but I haven't had the opportunity to furnish it, not even a bed."

I have no idea what to say. How do you respond to that?

Where did the carefree man I met in Kauai go?

"I'd like you to go shopping with me, since I have no idea what to put in my new house."

That makes me laugh. Me, an interior decorator? I would starve to death.

"I don't think I'm the right person for that. Why don't you ask your grandmother for help? She knows you well, she must know what you like."

"My grandmother is sick, she suffers from Alzheimer's. Some days she's fine, others not so much," he explains sadly. "Anyway, I want you to come with me."

How did I get into this mess? A minute ago we were talking about food, water, and weapons, now we're buying furniture for the house he bought because he's planning to settle down?

I have to put a brake on this train before it derails.

"Adrik, just take a look around, and you'll see that I have no idea about those kinds of things."

I indicate with a wave of my arms around the mostly empty apartment.

I have nothing but my beloved Nespresso, which prepares the best lattés on the planet, two wineglasses, and that's it. No, that's not quite true, I also have the pineapple cup he gave me in Kauai that I have not had the courage to use.

"I'm back to being Adrik again," he laughs. "So let's do this."

My subconscious betrays me. It's a double agent in this operation.

"That's not the point," I say. "I don't know anything about furnishing a house, or what kind of things you like."

"But you do know what I like." He hasn't finished the sentence and I'm already caught between his arms and the Formica countertop. "A dark-eyed, stubborn brunette with a sassy mouth."

I roll my eyes and he chuckles. "You can't decorate your house just based on that information."

It's absurd. This is an absurd conversation, this is all pointless.

"Of course I can," he replies playfully, his mouth finding my neck, tracing a path on my skin. "A couple of photos of you on each wall, preferably in that skimpy bikini you were wearing the day I met you."

My face turns red, and for the record, I don't blush easily.

"Then I wouldn't be able to come over to your house, not even once."

"That would be a shame," he replies, kissing my skin, making me shiver as I vibrate with his touch.

"It's late, Adrik, we have to finish this damn work, and we haven't even started on the route calculations yet. There are so many numbers that I think I'm going crazy."

This is my very own version of Netflix & no chill.

"You're in a hurry, how long did you say this course is?"

"Sixteen weeks," I reply. "More than OCS, minus the physical training."

He makes a face...

"At least I didn't go to the academy," he says.

"Yeah, plebe year is hard, even being a fourth class Midshipmen isn't child's play. I had some privileges, being one of the class's top students."

"Nothing could be worse than boot camp, and of course you were."

"Because my last name, you mean?"

"I believe you can achieve anything you put your mind to."

We get back to the sheets in front of us, I still have a few hours of study waiting for me and he's not helping.

"If you want my advice, just trust yourself. If you want your staff to believe in you, then you have to start by believing in yourself, in the plans you've drawn up. You'll be a Lieutenant Commander in a few months, and that means taking command, Jordania. You will be the one making the decisions."

"What about planning for the unexpected?" I ask.

"That's always a possibility, but if you've assessed the risks and calculated the options, the probabilities will always be in your favor."

We return to the figures, the spreadsheets, and plans, but the thread of tension that pulls me toward him is still there. Shortening the distance, approaching me, preventing me from escaping to a safe place.

"You know I'm going to want something in exchange for all this, right?" He smiles.

Of course, nothing in this life comes free, everything has a price.

"You're not playing fair," I rebuke him.

"All is fair in love and war," he says. "You leave me with very few options."

Whatever is happening between us, I'm sure it's not about love.

"So tell me then, what is it that you want in exchange for your help?"

Adrik raises his eyebrows at my sharp tone.

"Go out with me, let me take you to a beautiful place."

"We already did that."

How could I possibly forget that night?

"Go out with me *again*," he insists.

"I don't date colleagues, much less a superior officer."

That is a rule that I'm not willing to break.

"You're not my subordinate, because I'm not *your* commander. Although I wouldn't mind giving you some orders."

Oh my, thinking about him being bossy with me, commanding my body…

Calling him *sir,* in private.

"It doesn't matter. You can argue the technicalities about the line of command, but those are my rules."

I see many things reflected in his smoky eyes, beginning with what happened at the stairs.

"Don't they say that rules were made to be broken?"

"Not mine," I reply.

"Just go out with me, Jordania. I want to spend more time with you."

"You had your chance in Kauai. Wasn't my fault you let me go."

His jaw tenses, he looks at me like he doesn't know what to do, strangle me or kiss me.

"I decided to give you some space that night. I went to your house the next morning looking for you, but no one came to the door."

"I had to go back to Honolulu, to pack everything up for my move."

Of course he doesn't believe my argument as he looks around the bare condo. Yes, I had very little to pack, but still.

"What is it that you're running from? Don't tell me you're a coward? What scares you so much?"

"I'm not afraid of anything," I insist, exasperated.

"Then go out with me."

He's back on the same path, this man is stubborn, hardheaded, and even more obstinate than me. We are talking about world class persistence.

"Go out with me on Friday." Here we go again. He's never going to give up.

"All right," I sigh, tired of his insistence. "We can go out on Friday."

And suddenly it seems like an eternity before I'll see him again.

"I'll pick you up at seven," he says, stroking my hair, catching me in the heat of his gray eyes, heavy with desire. "This time I'm taking you to a fancy place. I'm going to sweep you off your feet, you have been notified."

Unable to speak, I remain glued to my chair, bewitched by his presence, the confidence he exudes, his determination.

"I gotta go, it's past midnight. You have to rest and I must be up at four. I have a very early exercise scheduled." Of course, like everyone else, now that he got what he wanted, he's off.

He closes his laptop and puts it away in his black leather bag.

As I get up to accompany him to the door, he doesn't miss the opportunity to catch hold of me, trapping my body with his.

I grab him by the forearms, intending to push him away, but instead find myself touching his warm skin, enjoying his closeness.

"See you tomorrow for dinner. Do you like sushi?" he says, kissing his way down my cheek.

"Tomorrow isn't Friday, Adrik," I point out breathlessly. My lungs are burning, why is it so warm in here?

"I just decided that I want to have dinner with you and I don't want to wait until Friday."

With those words, he gives me a dry kiss on the lips and departs, leaving me alone and trembling.

Anxious and wanting more.

Damn, he knows exactly what he's doing to me.

Rule # 7: Don't be afraid to make a risky move, or change tactics, but never cheat. A good opponent is one who keeps his hands clean.

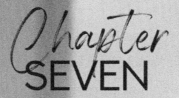

Chapter SEVEN

As soon as Adrik leaves, I check all the bolts. No, not the ones at the door, this place is quite safe, but the ones in my head as it seems I'm in danger of losing my reason, and along the way, my composure.

The first bolt, the one that protects my motives, remains in place, firmly closed. But the second, the one that protects my confidence, is beginning to cave in, looking like a lost cause. The ones guarding my heart seem to have gone for a walk, perhaps the pair of bums have decided to stay on the beaches of Hawaii.

Fuck, I'm screwed.

And not in the way I would like.

Of course, while I'm lying on my bed, looking at the white ceiling of my room, I repeat again and again that this man must have caffeine running through his veins since I find him so addictive. I can't get the Sandman to visit me, so I entertain myself by making a list of all the reasons why I must stand firm and not fall prey to the seduction of Commander Houston.

First and foremost is the danger of giving far more than I'm willing to let go of.

The second is that he said that the time has come for him to settle down, surely he'll be wanting some prissy lady, someone who knows how to cook, how to iron his uniform, and who would style her hair using inspiration from Pinterest boards. Someone neat and impeccable.

And that's not me. I'm nothing like that. I'm stubborn, loud, bossy, and a tomboy. I know how to efficiently handle a squad of men, but I don't have a clue about how to run a house, take care of children, all the traditional 'wifey' things. Zero percent wife material, that's me.

I've been there before, and right now, I'm happy being myself, I certainly don't want anybody telling me I need to change. Sure, I get that a relationship is about finding common interests and compromising, but from my experience I'm pretty sure I would find it too much of a compromise on my part.

My determination is the only thing I have left. I'm determined to reach my goals and I don't care how long it takes. Someday I'll be working at the Information Warfare Systems Command located here in San Diego. Yeah, life can be a bitch. So close, yet so far.

Someday, I'll be there developing solutions to the problems the force has.

Someday.

After all, dreaming is free.

And yet Adrik keeps coming back into my head. Despite telling myself over and over again that there is no future for us, it's just not possible, why does that man continue to sneak into my thoughts?

He's only interested in me because I am an intriguing new challenge, but as soon as he gets to know the real me, he'll find me no more interesting than the flagpole in the garden.

Besides, I'm very aware that Adrik is just as stubborn as I am, plus he's as persuasive as a canny fox, and just as elusive. If I was falling in love with him, I'd think he was perfect and wouldn't find any faults, would I?

Logic, Jordan, use logic.

I feed my rage and anger, reminding myself of all the hard times I went through in the past, the jealousy, the scenes, and even the abuse.

Of course, I would never allow it to happen again, but if an idiot like Glenn Sanders was able to hurt me so much, then Adrik Houston would tear me apart. My ex isn't even close to Adrik's shadow.

He asked me tonight why I'm so afraid and even though I denied it, the truth is I AM afraid. Scared shitless, if I'm being totally honest.

I force myself to leave my phone on its charger and not look up the Instagram profile of the cocky commander. As much as I want to know more about him, I have to resist the temptation.

God help me!

By the time dawn breaks, I feel almost twenty years older. As best I can, I hide the dark circles under my eyes with layers of concealer and prepare to start the day in my daily uniform—today I'm wearing pants—impeccable and well pressed as always.

Ah, the delights of not having to think about what to wear every day and having to deal with the closet full of nothing to wear.

Even running to the base with my black flats, I'm the last to arrive in the classroom, but fortunately the instructor of the day hasn't arrived yet, so I'm safe.

"Where are you staying?" Adrian Matthews calls out when he sees me arrive. "I'm sharing a condo at Dietz hall with Stephens. We're ready to hit the pool this weekend, so there will be a party on Sunday."

Ha! I have a condo all to myself, I want to brag, but I keep my mouth shut. I don't want to risk more gossip about my father's influence getting me nice lodging.

"We're going for drinks on Saturday." This time it's Anderson talking. "Are you up for it, Zanetti?"

Maybe this is what I need, a breath of fresh air. Hang out with other people, have fun.

And if along the way I get with someone who lowers my fever, so much better.

This damn drought is affecting me.

"You can't say no," says Grace, the other girl in the group. "My boyfriend just left so I need the distraction."

"I'm in," I assure them. "Where and when?"

"There's this place on India Street with good drinks and chill vibes. Saturday at nine, I'll text you the details."

"I'll be there."

Our instructor arrives and our free time is over. It's time to get serious, we have a lot of work pending.

Today we will be discussing navigation. When commanding a ship, although we have specialists in the crew, as commanders we still need a comprehensive understanding of the subject. Besides, our instructor has just warned us that we'll be starting some field practices in the facilities that the navy has in the north of the county. Apart from a short break to have a snack, the day is pretty full.

I've been so busy that I've barely had time to think about how I'm going to deal with another dinner with Adrik. At least I have the excuse of work, because I have more than enough to do and no doubt he will also have plenty to catch up with.

By the time I arrive back at my apartment, Adrik is already standing there waiting for me at the door, dressed casually in a white T-shirt and gray sweatpants, the masculine equivalent of wet t-shirts.

"You're early," I say instead greeting him.

He shrugs and lifts the paper bag with some red Japanese symbols printed on the front that he's holding in his left hand.

"I need fuel," he says, but in his eyes I see that he's not referring only to food.

"And I need a shower."

"Is that an invitation? I can rub your back, I'm pretty good at it, as well as rubbing other parts too." This man. I just roll my eyes at him in response.

He's impossible.

I search through my bag for the keys to the door, but before I can find them, an arm catches me, forcing me up against his hard body.

All of him is hard.

Of course Commander Houston has his big weapon pointing and ready for war.

Those gray sweatpants and their contents are too hot to handle.

The bag falls to the floor and I let myself go for the moment, for what I feel, what I want.

"Do you want me to kiss you, Jordania?" he murmurs, his mouth seeking a path on my neck.

In response, I wet my dry lips.

"You're not ready for it yet," he whispers, his breath caressing my ear, causing goosebumps. "Have you thought about me? I've been hard all day, thinking about all the things I want to do to you, with you. Dreaming about how it'll feel in the paradise concealed between your legs."

Uh huh, those words make my skin tingle and my center wet.

"Adrik…" I want to rebuke him, but only a soft groan comes out of my mouth.

In a gesture of unexpected tenderness, he caresses my face with great care, from my hairline, along my eyebrows— which he outlines with his fingers—my cheeks, until the tip of his index finger touches my lips.

I'm living one of the most sensual moments of my life, out in the corridor, where anyone can see us, with our clothes on and what's worse, I don't care in the least.

He's driving me crazy.

I can't stop being me, playful and sassy. I bite his finger gently and then lick it slowly, very slowly.

He growls in response. Mission accomplished. I smile, satisfied with myself. If he can tear down my walls, then I can also break down his defenses. The best line of defense is attack.

Tit for tat, Commander. Quid pro quo.

Minutes later, we enter the apartment and I leave him in the kitchen, taking care of the food. I urgently need a shower, my uniform is itchy and I want to wash away the tensions of the day, otherwise I won't be able to keep my eyes open for more than a few minutes. And although I want to focus on the man waiting for me, I also have tons of work to do, as I'm sure he does too.

I think I'm getting used to Adrik's way of treating me, and have to admit that if he didn't try to flirt with me, I would actually miss it. Our banter is quite fun and entertaining. The atmosphere is always charged with tension and electricity. It's exciting, like always having goosebumps.

"I was thinking," he says as we start eating the sushi. "What do you think about riding my bike over the weekend and crossing the border? I know a resort south of Ensenada, which I'm sure you'd like. It's beautiful, quiet, and at this time of year it won't be crowded with tourists."

"You have a bike here too?"

"Of course." He smiles, as if I'd just asked something obvious.

Luckily, I'd just swallowed what I had in my mouth, or I would have choked on a shrimp.

Has he never heard of the expression 'one step at a time'?

"I'm sorry," I tell him. "I have plans for Saturday. You forced me to go out with you on Friday, but that's it. One date, one night. Period."

"I didn't force you to go out with me. I was persuasive. There is a difference."

"Whatever. It is basically the same thing." Let's get back to the point. "I have no commitment with you other than the one date we made, which I will keep. But on Saturday I have other plans."

"Oh?" He raises an eyebrow.

I don't care if he doesn't like it, and I'm ready to add more fuel to the fire.

"As I was saying, on Saturday, my classmates and I are going out for drinks. They know a place on Indian Street with good drinks and chill vibes." I use Anderson's words.

"Tell me what time you're going, and I'll drive you," Adrik insists, rather than just politely offering.

"Don't be ridiculous," I say, not needing an escort. "I don't need you to drive me anywhere. I'm just going out with my fellow sailors. If I say I'm going by myself, it's because I'm going *by myself.*"

"Jordania, you just arrived in the city, you don't know anyone and you don't know your way around yet. If you get drunk, how will you get back home?"

"There are some yellow tin cans called taxis, in case you haven't heard. Or I could order a Lyft from my cell phone. Just drop it."

"Have you read the news lately? Do you have any idea how many women end up being abused, even kidnaped by those drivers?"

Oh my gosh, this overprotectiveness is exhausting. I'm a grown ass woman, as well as a fully trained member of the force.

I roll my eyes. "Don't be melodramatic. People take rides every day, and I'm a tough girl, I can see after my own safety. Your concern isn't necessary, thank you very much."

Steam virtually comes out of his ears.

"Jordania, don't even bother arguing with me because I'm taking you. What time shall I pick you up?"

He's way out of line. He isn't my father, or my brother, much less my boyfriend to think he can boss me around like this. I've had enough of that in this life and the next one too.

The only one that controls what I can or can't do is *me*.

"Pay attention carefully, Adrik Houston. I have no recollection of surrendering my free will to you, much less letting you control my whereabouts. I'm going out *by myself* with my colleagues, period."

Adrik stands there with his hands on his hips. Those arms are a distraction, but still…

"And how are you so sure you will get back home safely?" he demands, scowling angrily.

"If I can return in one piece from my first tour of the Persian Gulf, I think I can handle getting back from an innocent night out with my friends."

"There's nothing innocent about it." He glares at me. "Tell me, who's going to bring you home safe and sound?"

"I'm a big girl and I know my way back home. If I get drunk, I'll just ask one of the others to share the ride with me. After all, I'm not the only one who lives here."

"Oh yeah? Let's see, who could you share a ride with? Don't tell me it's going to be with that asshole Matthews, or better yet with Vargas, who probably will get you drunk so he can get into your pants."

He has invoked Medusa. Snakes and all. I wish I could turn him into stone. He would make a beautiful piece to decorate my empty condo.

"Look who's talking," I retort scathingly. "I know how to deal with idiots like them. After all, I've been doing it with you for several days."

He almost seems offended as he glares at me incredulously.

"I'm not like them."

"Says who?"

Facts not words.

"Jordania, I'm telling you you're not going out alone on Saturday," he warns.

Who the fuck does he think he is? Last time I checked, my father lives in DC, and I don't need or want another man attempting to take control of my life.

"I'm going to go out and there's nothing you can do to stop me."

I get up from the stool where I was sitting and walk to the balcony. He follows and grabs me by the elbow, then I see him raising his hand.

And at that moment everything comes back to me like an avalanche.

The shouts, the insults, feeling small, and insignificant.

The way I was belittled despite my efforts to please him, for trying to be the girl he expected me to be. Perfect, smiling, quiet. Undemanding yet attentive. And always, *always*, ready to jump into bed with him.

I cringe at Adrik's touch, anticipating the pain.

"No, please," I plead. "Don't hit me."

Adrik is instantly paralyzed by my words, his anger subsides immediately.

"Jordania," he says quietly, while I tremble like a leaf in a gale. "What the hell happened to you, baby? Who hurt you?"

That's the thing with the past.

You can run, you can hide, but if you don't deal with it, it will always come back to haunt you.

Rule # 8: Good manners will never go out of style. My grandfather taught me that a woman shouldn't be touched, not even with a rose petal.

Chapter EIGHT

We have all made mistakes, some small, some huge. Of the first I have made many, of the latter, more than I would like to admit. One in particular is the one that haunts me.

Since then, the shadows chase me, silent, dark, stuck to my body. I try to surround myself with light, but it just gets stronger, more visible. It never disappears, it's always there, like a scar that not even the best makeup can hide.

Because it's a ghost that hovers in my head, whipping chains, opening, and closing doors in my head, tormenting me when I least expect it.

The murmur of those words that hurt me so much.

Hussy.

Whore.

Easy.

Although I have decided to live my life by my own rules, the wound is still there, only half healed, suppurating, burning inside.

Getting deeper and deeper.

That's why I no longer believe in fairytales. When the sun rises, the demons remove their masks, and the magic ends.

Prince Charming turned into a real man and Cinderella had to deal with him.

Not the hero.

By sheer luck, mine revealed his true colors before I made an even more serious mistake. Even so, it remains my secret. I have only told one person what happened. Only Casper knows the truth and to this day he's the sole guardian of my secret. If my father had known, he would have reacted by getting his hands dirty with blood and I'd never want that. There was already more than enough violence, so it would only have added further aggravation to a very unpleasant situation.

And now there is him. Adrik.

He's still here. His voice is like a soft murmur calling me, while I swim in a sea of tears.

"Jordania, look at me, talk to me," he whispers.

His arms wrap around me, and I let myself be comforted by his soft touch, by the warmth of his body, by his smell.

By his strength.

Gradually the tremors stop and the crying ceases.

"Annie," I murmur, surprising even myself. "That's what he called me."

"Who?"

"My fiancé. I accepted his proposal. I was going to marry that man."

"What happened?" he asks, cuddling me against his chest, firm yet gentle at the same time. "What did that bastard do to you?"

The muscles in his chest tense, yet I don't feel fear. He's my safe haven.

Adrik is not going to hit me, the object of his anger is someone else and, as far as I know, he's far away from here.

At first, I wished he would rot in hell, but after a lot of time and reflection—and tears—I let the anger go and forgave him.

Forgiven but not forgotten.

That gave me peace.

"Glenn seemed everything a girl could hope for. On paper, at least, he was the perfect man many girls dream of, complete with his panty melting white uniform and everything. Tall, blond, and very polite, and from a family with a great tradition in the military. My father was on cloud nine."

"I bet he was," Adrik says wryly.

Little did I know there was something hidden under the guise of a cultured man.

"I was so naïve, I fell in love with him at first sight. Casper introduced him to me, and we fell madly in love. I was young, inexperienced, and fresh to the world after escaping from my father's hawk surveillance. Glenn was the first man I allowed to touch me, the first man I ever made love to, and at first, I felt I was the luckiest girl in the world. Until I got to know him better."

Adrik is silent, and in the empty apartment only the quiet sound of our breathing can be heard, but I can almost hear his heart beating furiously, a drum calling for war. His arms surround my body to comfort me, and I can feel each of his reactions, knowing that I'm finally revealing everything I've held in for so long that has been blackening my soul.

"He was handsome and rich, born with a silver spoon in his mouth, but Glenn surprised me as our relationship progressed. Every day he became more demanding, more insecure, wanting to know where I was at all times. My cell phone kept going off all day long, even when I was at work or training. You know the kinds of problems that can lead to, but if I didn't answer, he got furious and made me feel terrible for ignoring him."

"Motherfucker," Adrik murmurs as his hands travel soothingly up and down my back. His touch is no longer sensual, it's comforting and exactly what I need from him right now.

"Glenn was the air I breathed, my whole world, but nothing I ever did was enough to satisfy him. At first, there were comments about my clothes, my hair, even my makeup. He asked his mother to give me advice and because I was a stupid girl back then, I gladly accepted. Every time I would put on one of the outfits she'd chosen for me, I felt suffocated by the layers of fabric, as my own personality got blurred, but at the time I thought that was proof of my love and devotion."

"He wanted to change you, the whiny motherfucker."

"Slowly, I started distancing myself from all my friends, except Casper, who was also his best friend. I stopped going out, or going to parties without Glenn, even though I've always enjoyed going dancing. But Glenn would turn into a beast if I dared to go out somewhere without him. At first they were scenes full of supposed sadness, and then he'd shout at me, accuse me of cheating on him with other men, with my classmates. In his eyes, anyone who spoke more than a couple of words or dared to smile at me was a potential suitor. In the end, even his family was judging me, and I think he even got to my father. It was horrible, I felt judged, sentenced. Each time our discussions became more heated, until in the end…"

Adrik takes a deep breath before I finish my sentence.

"In the end he hit you."

Shit, that was the worst part. The part that hurts the most, the one that I find hardest to admit.

"We'd just gotten engaged, you know? He gave me a rose-shaped platinum ring, a family heirloom, most likely picked out by his mother. He said that I was his delicate little flower, although I never wanted him to treat me that way. I wanted to be his wife, his partner, his equal."

"But he didn't see you that way." It's a statement, not a question and he's right.

"He wanted me to become someone that I'm not, a carbon copy of his mother. And it was hard, because although I loved him, I couldn't bear it, I couldn't live like that, certainly not long-term, because I believe that marriage is for life."

"Did you break up with him immediately?"

"No," I say, remembering what happened after the first slap. "Casper had to mediate between us. Glenn was depressed and threatened to end his life. He was desperate to win me back, bringing dozens and dozens of red roses, crying, and apologizing down on his knees. I had so many doubts, because I still loved him, and wanted to be his wife. He promised me that he would change, that he loved me for who I was, for what I meant to him."

"And you believed him?"

"I believed him," I admit, though I'm ashamed.

"After I forgave him, the first few weeks were great. We started focusing on planning the wedding. That summer we were set to finish at the academy and become officers, so we set the date for before Thanksgiving. Using both his family's contacts and mine, we got posted in Connecticut, because Glenn dreamed of being part of the scuba diver squad and I complied with what he wanted."

I was going to give up my dreams for him, and in the long run, I would have left to dedicate myself to the home, to raising the children that surely would have come after the wedding.

"My father bought a house for us and we began to furnish it, but of course my mother-in-law had to stick her nose in our business. It began with hints, then little suggestions, gifts, until she was totally imposing her wishes on us. I told Glenn it had to stop and after he agreed to talk to her, things calmed down, at least for a short while."

"When did you finally break up?"

"Two weeks before the wedding," I sigh, knowing this is the worst part. "I had an appointment with the jeweler to pick up Glenn's wedding band, but I couldn't start my car. Of course the first thing I did was call him, but I couldn't get ahold of him, so a guy who was passing by offered to help, he jump started my car's battery with his."

"Let me guess. The fucker came and found you and he wasn't happy?"

"Yes, he found us," I admit. It was a horrible scene, and if I close my eyes, I can still feel his fingers on my arm and his hands on my hair. "The poor guy got scared and called the police."

"Did you file a complaint against him? Did you tell your father?"

"No," I confess, and shame fills my chest. "The officer who came to take my statement told me, among other things, that if I hadn't opened my legs, my boyfriend wouldn't be so angry."

"What a fucking idiot," Adrik growls. "Why didn't you do anything about it? It just doesn't seem like you."

"I'd barely turned twenty-two that summer, I still had a lot to learn, plus his family was very influential," I sigh. Glenn threatened me with things I prefer not to repeat, and I was afraid he would keep his word. "But after that afternoon, I was done. I couldn't do it anymore, because I knew that if I gave in, it would lead to my end. My father was not very happy when I told him that I was cancelling the wedding, and the scandal was terrible. I wanted to hide from everything and everyone. All I wanted was to bury my head in the sand like an ostrich and never see anyone again. Maybe I was being a coward, but I needed some space."

"You weren't a coward," he says, hugging me tighter. "You did what you had to do."

"I asked for a transfer to the Pacific fleet, and with my father's help, I ended up in Hawaii, which has been my operations center since then."

"A circumstance that was beneficial for me," he laughs.

I remain where I am, I don't have the strength to move. I want to stay here, safe in his arms, feeling him close, listening to him breathing, and the rhythm of his heart.

"Do you want something to drink?" he asks after a while. We're out on the balcony and it's getting chilly. "I put a couple of beers in the fridge."

Although I know that alcohol isn't the answer, the idea of doing something relatively normal with him after telling him my ugly past sounds perfect. Plus it'll change the vibe that flows between us.

We walk back inside the apartment in silence, which is oddly comforting.

"Are you hungry?" I ask, looking at the bags standing on my counter.

"Forget the food, how are you feeling now?" Adrik asks as he takes a long drink from his can and I do the same before answering.

We are standing in my kitchen, neither of us wants to sit back on the stools and there aren't any other places to sit.

"Like I've just undergone an exorcism," I laugh the matter off, although the truth is that I'm exhausted. Exhausted, yet liberated. I just removed a huge weight from my shoulders. And of course it was with him. What does he have that makes me open up to him in this way?

"Thank you for trusting me," he murmurs. "And I want you to know that my lips are sealed."

"I do know and I appreciate it."

"But I can't help feeling angry, pissed off, and frustrated on your behalf. I wish you would tell me who that bastard is, so that I could find him and then dismember him, *slowly*. I have a couple of ideas of what I'd like to do with him, because that man deserves hell."

I open my mouth to scold him, to tell him that's not what I want, but I don't get the chance. Adrik raises his hand, asking me to let him finish. "But as you said, what you lived through was violent enough, so now it's time for you to heal, to look to the future, to be happy."

"That's what I want. To be happy, to be me, to live by my own rules."

"Following your own rules while being a Navy officer, you're such an enigma, Jordania Zanetti," he says with a smile.

"That's why I can't allow you to set rules for me, Adrik. I've been through that once and I don't want to go back there."

He looks at me for a couple minutes, as if thinking about what to say next.

"Jordania, I don't want to control you, that was never my intention. I'm just worried about your safety, about your well-being."

But that's how it starts, as I know all too well.

"No, Adrik, your intentions might be good, but it still is controlling behavior. You and I are… fuck I don't even know what we are."

Frenemies? Enemies with benefits?

He looks at me, raising one of his dark eyebrows.

"It's a slippery slope. If I give in to this, I'll end up giving in to everything else and I don't intend to stumble twice on the same stone."

He closes his eyes before answering. "Jordania, I hear what you're saying, *but still.*"

"These are my rules, Adrik. This is my life and I will like to live it my way. I will never let my spirit be changed again, or let anyone steal my joy."

"I can assure you that I like you just the way you are," he says and his admission unsettles me.

But…

"Adrik, you told me you want to settle down, so obviously you're looking for a woman that fits in with those plans. Now, you may have noticed that I'm not very feminine or what some would call wife material. Confession—I've never invited you to dinner because I have no idea how to even boil water," I admit. "And let's not get started on babies. I've never been around kids, they're scary creatures to me, and I wouldn't know what to do with one. So I'm clearly not the type of woman you're looking for."

"Don't make decisions based on those assumptions. I'm not a boy, I'm a thirty-eight year old man, and I know what I want, Jordania Zanetti."

"It makes no difference," I state, taking another sip of my beer. "You'd want to change me, otherwise we'd end up killing each other. I'd become a pale reflection of who I really am, a ghost of what I want to be, because a man like you would consume me."

"Your essence could only be diluted in a sea of weakness and I'm not a weak man."

Taking my face in his broad hands, he tilts my head just enough to be able to look me in the eye.

"Just get to know me, let me get to know you, that's not too much to ask for, is it?" he murmurs, gently stroking my cheeks.

I close my eyes and suddenly have a tremendous urge to cry. If I allow myself to do as he asks, I'll end up dropping to my knees, begging him to marry me, and take me to his little townhome, where we will live unhappily ever after.

"Give me a chance, Jordania, go out with me," he insists. "Go out with me, not because I forced you to, go out with me because you want to."

"Adrik …" I murmur, almost ready to surrender.

"Go out with me, let me show you what it is to be with a real man."

His mouth is very close to mine, I can feel his lips brushing against mine, inviting me to taste them.

"Jordania…" he says again, as he gently kisses along my chin.

And here, ladies and gentlemen, is where it all comes crashing down.

"Yes," I answer, feeling that those three letters, a simple word, just sealed my destiny.

Rule # 9: Let her know that in between your arms, all her dreams can come true.

Chapter
NINE

"Do you want to work for a while?" I ask Adrik after finishing the second can of beer.

"I don't really feel like it. Do you?"

"Not really. What do you want to do then?" I ask, looking at the empty apartment.

Please, don't say go to bed, pretty please.

"Let's go for a walk, just to the docks and back." Phew, we are safe.

It sounds like the perfect idea. To be honest, at the moment the last thing I want to do is to calculate, estimate and so on, and even less to start reading entire volumes of diplomatic treaties.

"The weather is starting to change, it's chilly out here."

He is right, my light cardigan is barely keeping me warm.

"Resorting to talking about the weather now, Commander?" I say, teasing him a bit.

"It's good to know you're feeling better," he replies. "As much as I like offering a shoulder to cry on, I prefer the sassy, smart-mouthed Jordania."

"Sorry. I'll make sure not to cry in your presence ever again."

"There you go again, twisting my words," he scolds me. "What I meant was that I don't like to see you cry, I get a knot in my chest."

"I think you're not used to dealing with women, at least not when they're upset."

"You are kind of right," he admits. "My grandmother is usually cheerful, even if she barely recognizes me, and I didn't know my mother."

"I'm sorry," I tell him. "I imagine it's hard for you to deal with all of that, and for your grandfather too."

"He loves her fiercely, and even with nurses around at all times, he still takes care of her, and cooks all her meals."

"Are they your father's parents?"

"Yes," he sighs. "My father is a mess, even at his age he's still a brat. One day he took me to their home and just left me there."

Jesus!

"Maybe that was the best gift he could ever give to you. If he isn't a grounded man, at least he showed you how much he cares by leaving you in a place he knew you will be safe and cared for."

"Maybe…" he replies, his hands in his sweatpants pockets, his gaze fixed on the path ahead.

"My mother died two days after I was born. I only have some pictures and a couple of stories my father has told me," I confide to him. "I didn't know her and yet I miss her every day."

He turns and focuses on me.

I want to comfort him and at the same time be comforted by him. I don't like to think of him hurting, because I get how he feels. He just talked about living without memories and I'm living with no memories too. My father talks very little about my mother, I guess that's his way of coping with the pain.

"I left you speechless, huh?"

"I was just thinking about my mother," he replies. "We share the same loss, Jordania. But life is about more than that, and I want to share mine with you."

I get a lump in my throat. I need to change the subject immediately.

This has been an intense night, for both of us.

"How did you end up in the Navy?"

"I had no money for college and, although everyone advised me I should go, I hated the thought of getting into debt with student loans. So after weighing all my options, I decided that joining the force seemed like a good idea, and definitely preferable to getting into all kinds of trouble because I had too much free time."

"And how did you become an officer, when one of the requirements is to either go to the academy or go to school?"

"Well, it was by a stroke of luck really. I started out as an enlisted sailor, but then I got recommended for an officer training program, and the rest is history."

"Do you really believe in luck?"

"I believe you make your own fate. It wasn't by chance that I got selected. My philosophy is that if I'm going to do something, I do it to the very best of my ability. So I worked really fucking hard, and that's what got me noticed."

"What about the parties and living the crazy life?"

He laughs and I love the hoarse, loud sound.

"That's not for me. I saved all my money and bought a new home for my grandparents, and then I bought one for myself, since I'm fortunate enough to have a steady income with good benefits."

I think there's more to this than meets the eye, but I don't want to push him.

"You're different from most guys."

"I'm just like any other guy, Jordania, with defects and virtues. Maybe with a lot of the first and a few of the second."

"The balance is not so bad," I tease him. "You're easy on the eye, just about bearable, so it's not so bad spending time with you."

We both laugh.

"Feels as if this is the first time we've talked, right? That we've *really* talked," he sighs.

I know what he means. It's weird how you can talk for hours with a person while actually saying nothing of substance.

"Well, the other times you were just trying to impress me, to get into my pants."

He lets out a laugh.

"I still want to get into your pants," he acknowledges. "But it's more than that. I want to see where this goes between us, how far we can take it."

Here we go again.

"Adrik, I'm not the one you need," I tell him. "I'm not the woman you're looking for, and if you keep insisting that I am, it'll be a waste of time, and one of us will end up getting hurt."

We're interrupted by a couple of officers who greet us, then we continue walking without saying a word, until we reach an esplanade from which the bay can be seen.

"A penny for your thoughts," he murmurs, breaking the silence that surrounds us.

"Thank you for tonight, Adrik," I say, admiring his face, the strength of his jaw, the intensity of his gaze. "However this ends, it has been liberating, so thank you."

"Jordania, I meant what I said, and I don't want to hurt you," he promises and I believe him, I really do believe him.

"I know, but many times we hurt those who are important to us even if we don't mean to. It's inevitable."

"Just trust me when I say that not everyone is the same."

"I don't know about that, Adrik," I say. "All I know is that I have to protect myself, and my rules are what keep me safe."

"Then it's time for you to get some new rules."

Coming from his lips, that sounds like a fact. And also a warning.

To my surprise, I slept better than I have in a long time, and in the morning I wake up feeling fresh.

When there's a knock on the door, I assume it must be him, the stubborn man. He's already made it a habit to invite himself to dinner every night and now he also wants me to accompany him to breakfast?

I open the door ready to release a long string of curses, when to my surprise, I find my best friend's worried face.

"Casper," I greet him. "What are you doing here?"

"Can I talk to you for a minute?"

At least he has the manners to ask permission, so different from another man I know.

"Sure," I answer, standing back to allow him to enter and then closing the door behind him. "Have you had breakfast yet? I have cereal, or do you want coffee?"

"Don't worry, I'm fine, thank you."

"What brings you here so early?" I ask him and he laughs. I know him well, and he wouldn't come to visit me at this time if it wasn't something important.

"Didi, I don't want to interfere in your life, but I'm worried about you."

Oh fuck. What happened?

"I don't understand, what do you mean?" I ask, puzzled.

"I don't know where to start, it's a sensitive issue."

"Well, at the beginning would be good. What is it that you want to tell me?"

He gives a hollow laugh.

"Direct as always," he says. "Well, last night a colleague called me quite late, and told me that he saw you with Commander Thunder, and it was not the first time either."

"With whom?" I ask, because I don't recognize that name.

"With Houston, with Commander Adrik Houston."

Ah right. Of course, this is like a schoolyard, gossip spreads like wildfire.

"Wow, that didn't take long," I say, dropping onto one of the stools next to the breakfast bar, incidentally, the only place where one can sit.

"Didi, you're my best friend, and I'm worried about you."

I understand he's my friend, but why should he be concerned?

"I still don't get the message, Casper, you'll have to spell it out for me."

"He isn't the right man for you, Didi. You're a great woman and officer, but you're vulnerable and I don't want that... *that guy* hurting you."

"Explain," I say, although it sounds like an order.

"I don't know him personally, but they say he's a womanizer and a player."

His description of Adrik doesn't add up to me, are we talking about the same person?

Casper studies me to gauge the effect of his words before he continues.

"Apart from having a very bad reputation with his crew, which is why they gave him that nickname, they say he's tough, insensitive, and demands more than he is willing to give. Did you know that's why they brought him to the base? They're evaluating his performance, and the rumor is that he's likely to be discharged."

I still can't believe he's talking about the same man who held me last night while I was crying and scared to death. Adrik is not like that. This doesn't sound like the person who listened to me and also shared such personal details about his own life.

It can't be the man who told me about his grandparents, about his beginnings as a sailor, about his hopes.

He can't be the same man who asked for the opportunity to win my trust.

"Casper, are you sure about what you're saying?" I ask. "Maybe you're mistaken, are your sources reliable?"

"Jordania Marie Zanetti, do you think I would come to your house this early if I wasn't sure of what I was telling you?"

Well, not really, no. Even so…

"I just find it hard to believe," I admit to Casper. "It must be a mistake, I'm sure of it."

"Didi," he says in exasperation as he scratches his head, where the hair is so sparse his bald pate is plain to see. "Do your own research, speak to whoever you want. Just ask around if you don't trust me enough to take my word for it."

That hurts and I'm sure that he's hurt too. Casper is my friend, he's been my confidant for years, the one person who has been with me through thick and thin. However annoying he can be at times, I know that his friendship is sincere and his concern is genuine.

"I'm sorry, Casper, I didn't mean to be rude," I murmur. "It's just that this is all so unreal. Adrik has behaved in such a considerate way, that..."

"Because he's an excellent actor," he growls. "But once he gets what he wants from you, then you'll get to see his true colors."

The truth is that Adrik has always been upfront about what he wants from me, he's never hidden the fact that he wants to take me to bed. I understand that very clearly, but we have also talked about so many other things, and suddenly the idea of that person vanishing into thin air like mist makes me desperately sad.

Why the fuck do I care so much?

God, this went from bad to worse.

"I don't know what to think," I sigh.

It hurts me to admit that although I've been keeping up my defenses, Adrik has made a dent on them because he's different, or at least he made me believe he was different.

"Please, just tell me you're going to be careful," Casper asks as he puts his hand over mine. "Didi, after what happened with Sanders, I wouldn't want to see you get hurt again. This guy, Houston, has a bad reputation, and he would tear you apart in the blink of an eye without hesitation."

"Casper, but..."

"Promise me, my dear friend," he persists. "I'm worried about you, so promise me that you're going to cut ties with Houston. He's bad news."

"People can change," I protest in Adrik's defense.

"Not in his case, that guy is just a wolf in sheep's clothing. Don't let him fool you, Jordan. After the bad experience with your ex, I thought you would know better."

"I didn't forget, that experience will always remain with me, Casper." Nothing's ever been the same since then.

"Then cut all contact with Houston and send him to hell. If you want to go out and have fun there are many things we can do, you know I'm always here for you."

My head is spinning, that's all I know right now.

"It's a lot of information to process." I rub my brow in a vain attempt to ease the tension.

"Do you want to go out for dinner tonight?"

"No, thank you. I'm tired, the classes are really intense, and apart from that, I have a lot of work to catch up on."

"Remember that I love you, Didi, and that I only want what's best for you."

"I know, Casper, and I appreciate it."

I smile wanly, still finding it hard to accept what he just told me. This can't be true, can it?

"Do you want me to take you somewhere, give you a lift?"

"That's not necessary, thanks. I already bought a car."

"Wow." He frowns. "This is news to me. Why am I only now finding out by pure chance, why didn't you call and tell me?"

Because I was too busy thinking about Commander Thunder...

"Everything has been happening so quickly, I've been so busy I've barely had time to even sleep," I apologize.

Why am I apologizing?

"Well then, I won't take up any more of your time," he says, heading for the door. "Just don't be a stranger, don't wait so long to call me next time."

Then before I can think it through, I say the first thing that pops into my head.

"Listen, on Saturday I'm going out for drinks with my colleagues, would you like to come?"

"Sure, I'd love to. Call me and we'll arrange the details."

He kisses me on the cheek and then leaves me wrapped in a whirlwind of doubts.

I know Captain Nolan is a brilliant man, and a highly decorated officer and that he's speaking about important matters, but I'm incapable of listening to a single word he's saying.

So, after our short lunch recess, I excuse myself, giving him some lame excuse about feeling sick.

We sailors are forged by the sea, men and women with a backbone of steel, but I do look terrible today, so after a brief reprimand, he allows me to leave.

I walk to the covered parking lot, but I don't want to go home. I want to be alone. I don't want to give explanations or reasons to anyone.

I drive downtown mindlessly. I really don't know the city, I just go with the flow of cars. Thank God my tank is full, so I can drive for hours.

After a while, I park my car in front of a cute bakery and go inside. It's after the lunch rush, so the place isn't that busy.

The place has a rustic cozy vibe, it's like a farmhouse turned into a bakery. 'The Sweet Tooth' is written on a blackboard on the far wall over the counter, along with the menu.

"Hey, good afternoon, what can I get for you today?" asks a pretty brunette, wearing a cute dress with bows on the shoulders and a checkered apron. "We offer a military discount, to thank you for your service."

That's when I remember I'm still wearing my khakis.

"Well, I don't know," I confess, since everything on display looks amazing. "What do you recommend?"

"Oh girl," she laughs, her golden eyes lighting up. "My business partner is a very gifted baker, I could eat every single thing she bakes."

Well, let's live a little…

"Then please choose something for me—maybe a cinnamon bun?"

She smiles again.

"I'll fix you something lovely," she says. "Take a seat, I'll be with you in a few minutes."

I walk along in front of the windows, looking for a seat. I find an empty table for two in the far corner of the room.

After a short wait, she returns with a Reuben sandwich, two cupcakes, and a cinnamon bun. It all looks amazing, and my mouth is already watering.

"I don't think I can eat all of this."

"Then you can take them home." She smiles again. "A sweet treat always brightens a bad day."

"I hope that's true."

"It is," she replies, crossing her arms over her chest. "Promise. I'm Roselynn Holland, by the way. One of the owners."

"Jordania Zanetti," I say, giving her my extended hand.

"You can stay here as long as you want, I'll send you one of my special rose lemonades. You will love it, it's delicious."

"Fire away, I've never had one of those before."

She gives me a wink and leaves.

A smiling waiter comes over with a mason jar full of a pink drink beautifully decorated with a lemon slice.

People come and go, but I barely notice. After an hour, I've devoured every single crumb on my plate.

Roselynn comes back with a knowing smile on her lips.

"Feeling better?" she asks.

"You were right, the food is delicious." That's true, this might be my first time here but I'm sure it won't be the last. "You can count on me as a loyal customer from now on."

"I'm glad to hear that." She tries to smile but then her face becomes pale and wrinkles as if she were in pain.

"Are you feeling well?" Maybe I should call a doctor, or an ambulance? "Please take a seat."

"Yeah, sorry, I'm pregnant and this kid is already killing me," she admits as she sits down next to me, chuckling. "I have low blood sugar, so I get dizzy easily. I often forget to eat."

"Says the girl who owns the best bakery in town."

The color begins to return to her face.

"My husband says the same thing, so don't be on his team. Show some gender support, gal."

That makes me laugh.

I lift my hands in defeat. The same waiter who brought me the lemonade comes over with a glass of water, plus a plate with grapes, a slice of pineapple, and half a kiwi for her.

"I'm glad you're feeling better now," she says after a while.

"I could say the same thing about you."

"You want to talk about it?" she asks, before continuing. "Don't tell me some dumbass came to you with the ol' 'it's not you, it's me'. I swear that's the greatest hit in the history of mankind."

This time I laugh, hard.

"I don't know, I guess I feel a bit silly. I mean, I barely know this man, but he has turned my world upside down. He's really determined about wanting me, and his persistence drives me crazy," I confess, then suddenly feel guilty. "I'm sorry, I shouldn't be taking up your time like this when you have a business to take care of."

She puts her elbows on the table, giving me a stare.

"I'm a meddler, as my husband calls me. I can't help myself. I want people to be happy."

"You're doing a great job, this place is wonderful. I'm sure all your customers leave feeling way better."

"So, come on, tell me. Is this guy giving you the runaround?"

"Au contraire, this time it's *me*. This man scares the shit out of me. I don't need a man to feel good about myself or look after me. But he's so... so him, and I can't stop thinking about him, I feel overwhelmed by his presence even when he's not around."

"Girl, you're in trouble. The *best* kind of trouble."

Oh my… I'm not sure if this girl is a meddler, a tea sipper, or the tooth fairy, but I still tell her everything. About Adrik, about Casper's warning.

"Men are God's weirdest creation," she says. "Life would be way easier if they could actually communicate with us, but they have this stupid idea in their thick skulls about having to take care of us, protect us, and treat us like porcelain dolls. I mean, I don't want to be mistreated by anyone, but gosh…"

"I know what you mean."

"Talk with him, Jordania. I think he deserves the chance to give you his side of the story."

I guess she's right.

"In the end if you decide it's not going to work, at least you know you gave him a chance. Be fair and listen to him. Trust me, I had to learn this the hard way."

I keep my mouth shut, making no comment.

"Can I just ask, why are you paying so much attention to this other guy, your friend?" she asks and I smile, but it's a sad one.

"Because I know Casper means well, he's my only real friend and he's trying to take care of me."

"Are you sure? Like *really* sure?" she replies, looking me straight in the eye. Fuck, what is she getting at? "I think you're creating a storm in a teacup. You said you want to live your life under your own rules, so why are you following this guy's orders? He's clearly manipulating you."

"Why do your questions have to be so insightful?" This conversation is turning out to be a bit scary, the doubts she's putting in my head.

"Because I'm smart." She grins shamelessly. "And sorry if I'm going too far, but I think your friend Casper might be a little in love with you and he's jealous."

That makes me gasp, it can't be true.

"Casper isn't jealous," I reply defensively. "And he isn't in love with me, he's like a brother from another mother."

"If you say so," she says skeptically, lifting her dark eyebrows. "Anyway, you should talk with your guy, even if all you want to do is hit him in the head. I'm sure he has a story to tell. Everybody does."

Roselynn gets up and leaves, and I'm more confused than ever.

Sure, we need to talk but first I have some anger to release.

I arrive home to see Adrik's figure in the hallway of my apartment, I'm ready to fight.

I want answers and the night won't be over until I get them.

At any price.

Rule # 10: Be humble to recognize your mistakes, but do not underestimate your success. May honesty always be your banner.

Chapter
TEN

"I hope you're hungry." He greets me with a smile as I approach. "Tonight I brought pasta and salad from this famous place in Little Italy."

He looks so damn lickable, wearing another tight t-shirt with the letters NAVY on it, dark jeans, and hiking boots. He salutes me by lifting the brown bag he's carrying in his left hand, bringing it close to me. It smells divine and, although my mouth is watering, I remain still, there are more important things than food.

Like my integrity, for example.

"Good evening, *Commander Thunder,*" I greet him as I arrive at the door of my apartment.

He gives me a look, a mixture of anger and confusion.

"Where did you hear that name?" he asks in a harsh tone.

"It's one of the many things being said about you around the base."

He looks more and more upset by the second.

"Since when do you pay attention to gossip, Jordania?" Shit, he's really pissed off, but get ready, *Thunder*, because that makes two of us.

"Since I'm involved in it," I reply equally dry.

"Let's go in," he orders. "I don't want us to have this conversation out in the hall."

He takes the keys from my hand and opens the door himself, as if my house was his conquered territory.

Suddenly, my condo seems smaller and darker than before, as if it has been transformed into a cave.

"What do you want from me?" I ask, as I put my briefcase and handbag down on the counter.

"You know the answer to that," he replies immediately. "I've always been transparent with you."

"You want a quick fuck? I know that part," I reply bitterly. "But I want to know what else it is you want."

"You already know."

His short answers are pissing me off.

"No, you fucking moron, I don't know anything," I yell at him, not caring who can hear me. "You asked me to trust you, but how can I?"

His face is red with anger and frustration, his eyes the color of hard steel.

"You should know better than to pay attention to the ridiculous nonsense you hear around the base."

My fists are clenched tightly by my side.

"Ridiculous?" I scoff. "How can you tell me it's ridiculous?"

My self-control is hanging by a very thin thread.

"It's all lies," he insists. "If you would just calm down, then I'll happily tell you everything you want to know."

My body is shaking with rage.

"I don't feel like calming down," I shout. "Not when you've been making a fool of me."

"Jordania, if you're like this we're not going to be able to talk rationally like two reasonable adults."

Don't fuck me off with that poor old excuse.

"Reasonable adults? Us?" I don't know why that sounds insulting. "You mean a womanizer with his latest chick?"

"You aren't just the latest chick," he argues.

"You want to play silly games?" I tell him. "Well, I have news for you, Houston. Nobody gets to play around with me."

"Unless they follow your damn rules," he states, his voice rising a little.

"Even then I don't allow it," I state. "No one messes with me!"

"Well, Lieutenant Zanetti, since you've already declared yourself the winner, why not let me speak?"

"I'm not sure it's worth it. You'll only create a web of lies with some well-rehearsed speech."

He raises his eyebrows, clearly surprised and upset by my words.

"So you're going to act as my judge and executioner, right? *Well-rehearsed speech?*" he repeats. "Let's see, according to your informants, how many victims do I have under my belt?"

To be honest, I do not have the slightest idea and I don't want to know. It's too disgusting.

"Are you going to deny that you are the infamous Commander Thunder and that you got that nickname because of how you treat your sailors, as well as being a consummate womanizer?"

In his defense, he looks pretty offended at my words. As if I just slapped him, hard.

"This is all because you're jealous?"

"Don't fuck around with me. I'm not jealous, I just can't be with someone who'll only end up disappointing me."

He takes a couple of deep breaths before opening his mouth again.

"That nickname was an invention of Herrera, my second in command, because I'm energetic and bossy. I have *never* been harsh or unfair, not when I know how hard an enlisted has to work. I was in their place not so many years ago,

so I'm never unfair with them. As for the womanizer charge...
well, I never said I was a saint."

"So you don't deny it? You're the worst, Adrik
Houston."

"I don't deny I'm just a normal man, with a normal
man's needs." He shrugs. "But I've always been totally upfront
and honest with you. So, if you want to know something about
me, then ask! *Ask. Me!*"

"I'm not prepared to play games," I reply.

"And you think I am? *Shit!*"

"Shit is what you want my life to be," I rebuke without
giving an inch, wanting to tip this mess he has brought on his
head. "I have a career, a reputation to defend."

"And all that is so important to you, that you are not
able to see past these lies. But don't forget that I also have a
reputation and a career to defend, Jordania, after being in the
force for more than twenty years."

"Well, it seems you won't be in it for much longer. I'm
told you're only here because you're about to be discharged
from service."

He's paralyzed by my scathing comment, as if it's the
first he's heard about it.

"You are wrong." He shakes his head. "I've just
received an award and a pay rise."

Fuck, I'm so confused. My head is reeling.

"I'm sure I'm not," I stubbornly insist, lifting my chin. He tightens his jaw, I can see his neck muscles tighten, and a vein pulsing. "My sources are reliable."

Casper couldn't be lying. He couldn't be. Could he?

"Whoever it was, lied to you. If you want a reliable source, then ask me directly, Jordania. Fucking ask *me*!"

I know who I am, and most of the time I know exactly what men want from me. If I'm willing to give it to them, it's because we've laid out the cards on the table, without any cheap tricks between us. I've no intention of becoming anyone's inflatable doll.

"For what?" I shout, walking around the little kitchen in the apartment. "To give you the chance to put a blindfold over my eyes? What's the point of pretending there's something special between us when you and I both know it's a vile lie. Stop acting, man up, and be real!"

And those words break the dam.

Adrik cuts me off, pulling me against his body and taking one of my hands, pressing it against his fly, failing to cover the evident erection.

"God, you have no idea what you do to me," he growls, his mouth close to my ear.

"Don't try to distract me. I can't stand being lied to, I won't tolerate it," I tell him, my voice cracking.

Then Roselynn's words hit me. *He deserves a chance to give you his side of the story.*

"Do you think this is a lie?" he asks.

Fascinated, I caress his cock through the worn fabric of his pants, tracing the contour from top to bottom with my fingers, several times.

He's so thick, and hard. And long.

I'm dying to feel him moving between my legs.

"If you start this, you're going to have to finish it," he warns me.

In response, I find the zipper of his jeans and start to lower it. Adrik doesn't waste time. Still burning from the heat of our battle, he pulls my khaki shirt loose and then starts undoing the buttons.

His other hand slides up my back, going up, up, up to my neck, to the tight bun that I must style my hair in daily to undo it and then twines his fingers in my long dark hair.

There is nothing delicate or romantic going on here.

This is all about sex, fast and furious. What comes after that won't matter. He'll get what he wants, then he'll get out of my life as fast as he entered.

His hands cup my face and as he lowers his head so that our lips meet, mine open to receive his, warm and moist. Adrik tangles his tongue with mine and swallows my groans.

By some miracle, I manage to take off my blouse without tearing it, leaving my silk camisole and the edge of my lace bra in full view.

"My beautiful girl," he says, ogling at my chest with his eyes. "Beautiful Jordania."

He lowers first one silk strap and then the other, breaking down the barriers one by one that separate it from my heated skin. The slacks don't take long to fall to the floor, along with the rest of my uniform.

"I'm dying to taste you," he whispers seductively.

I'm naked and I don't care. Right now, all I know is I need this. I'll have time to think about this later—or to regret it—but for now all I want is something to calm this craving that grows within me and is consuming me.

Adrik lifts me up by the waist, ignoring my cry as I feel the cold countertop under my butt. His fingers caress my folds and I forget everything else. I'm wet and panting, ready for him.

I have imagined this many times, so many that I've lost count, but actually experiencing his fingers slipping into my heat far exceeds my expectations.

Adrik takes hold of my thighs and forces them apart so he can stand between them and cover my body with his. Next, his mouth leaves mine, to begin drawing a burning road southwards.

His fingers take care of my nipples, while he kisses my belly, playing with my navel. My hands fly to his head, wanting to press him closer to me, trying in vain to pull on his short cropped hair.

His tongue continues to travel, drawing maps around my body until it finally reaches the sweet place that impatiently awaits his attention.

"Adrik," I cry out when I finally feel his mouth there.

His fingers join in the action, increasing the pressure, the desire.

"You summoned the devil, Jordania, so get ready to meet him," he says, pulling away from me. I look at him with wild eyes, unable to speak. "You wanted to play with fire, right? So be prepared to get burnt when you find out who I really am."

Then he straightens up, turns around and leaves, quietly closing the door behind him.

I lie there, unable to process what just happened.

Damn you, Adrik Houston.

I need to get you out of my system as soon as I possibly can.

Thank God Saturday is nearly here, because I need to get drunk.

Rule # 11: A woman likes words, but words are meaningless without actions.

Chapter ELEVEN

How do you survive a heatwave? And this was not caused by global warming. I'm talking about the heat that shameless scoundrel left me suffering from on the kitchen counter.

I'm frustrated, pissed off and, shamefully, so horny.

Fucking bastard.

While resting between the sheets after a long, cold shower, I consider the idea of taking my BOB out just to release some tension, but I quickly discard the idea, knowing it won't satisfy my cravings as I'm not in the mood for a poor substitute.

Fuck, I'm so confused. A big knot of remorse squeezes my chest when I recall his hurt, angry eyes.

And the way he kissed me afterwards. The way he touched me.

By the time the sun starts peeking through the shades of my room, I've barely slept a wink.

I force my body out of bed and walk to take another shower since life doesn't stop just because this girl is a hot mess. Looking in the mirror, I can't even hold my own gaze. Madness still rages through my veins, I'm mad at myself, at him, and at this entire situation.

And let's not forget Casper.

There are so many questions swirling around in my head. *You should have at least listened to the man, Jordania, given him a chance to tell his side.*

I put my uniform on like it's the armor I need to conquer any battle ready to show the world how strong I am, knowing there's no going back now. And after the way he left last night, I'm pretty sure Adrik won't be coming back.

The knot inside me tightens again, making me gasp for air.

"Don't look at me that way." Dang, I resorted to talking to the pineapple on the kitchen countertop, like Tom Hanks in the movie *Cast Away*. Next thing you know, I'll be calling it Wilson.

I'm a lost cause.

I punish myself by eating horse food—please read high fiber dry cereal. Before leaving my apartment, I medicate myself with half a gallon of coffee. No, I'm not drinking it in the cup he bought me in Kauai. That one remains safely stashed in my dresser drawer.

A girl has to do what she has to do to survive.

This is the price I have to pay to be the heroine of my own story. Endure on my own.

I don't need more mementos around me. Although I swear the smell of his cologne still lingers in the enclosed space of my condo.

While leaving the lodging hall, I see Anderson and we walk together chatting a bit about the work we're doing this week and route estimations. Theoretically, each of us will be commanding a vessel, after mastering everything from performance statics to deployments, we are supposed to share our work with our fellow officers to discuss the results. We are getting ready for the next stage in our career as commissioned members of the service.

"We're going to have some field practice," our instructor announces, as he enters the meeting room assigned as our classroom. "We have a list of available vessels, and at the end of the instructions, we'll be going out into the open sea."

Everyone cheers as if they've been told we're going to a weekend long party, but I'm sure we won't have any spare time while training.

"Calm down," the captain orders. "It's not a vacation in The Bahamas."

See? I was right.

"We can only hope," someone shouts, Vargas I think. "We can dream, Captain."

"Not with the taxpayers' money," our instructor says very seriously.

"Captain, at least say we're going to have the opportunity to see Carr and Zanetti in a bikini."

The fucker.

"You might as well wish to see your grandmother in a bikini, idiot," my partner replies and I second the motion by nodding.

"If you want to see a Victoria's Secret angel, pay for them from your own money," I retort.

"I'd find big wings for you for the right deal, Zanetti," Vargas, the dumbass, replies.

"In your dreams, asshole. You are not worth the trouble."

Everyone whistles and boos, so the captain intervenes to bring order. We're supposed to be a group of responsible adults, part of one of the most powerful armed forces in the world, yet these guys are behaving like mindless idiots, showing their worst parts.

"I won't give you the name of your designated vessel until the day of the exercise. So you should get ready and plan very carefully for the days you'll be out on maneuvers. Everything must be taken into account, from water, to fuel and, of course, armament."

"Just like we're going to war," someone calls out.

"Ladies and gentlemen, this country has been at war for many years. Never forget that there are many enemies of freedom and that's why we have to always be prepared," the instructor insists firmly. "Remember, and remember it well, that the attack on Pearl Harbor happened in peacetime."

The conversation takes a serious turn and we all put ourselves back into full professional mode. It's true, we can never afford to play around or take chances with the lives of the people we protect. We can never forget, when we are the ones who are risking their skins, we must always be aware that an attack can happen at any time, the enemy won't be calling to advertise their intentions.

"Are we going out tomorrow?" Vargas asks at the end of the day, as we head down the stairs. "It has been an intense day, I need some distraction to lighten the mood, I'm looking for some action."

He thrusts his pelvis, making it clear what kind of action he's looking for.

"Don't be an idiot," Greg Anderson reprimands. "There are ladies here."

"You wouldn't be able to handle two, let's try one first," I challenge, because Carr has already left.

"Easy, tiger," Vargas laughs. "What do you say, see you tomorrow?"

"I'm in," I reply immediately. If anyone needs to relax, it's me. In addition, I should take advantage of the weekend to find a furniture store to look for at least the basics for my empty condo, the situation requires immediate intervention.

On Saturday, I spent most of the day cleaning the apartment, sending my uniforms to the dry cleaner, and looking for some furniture online, but without a measuring tape, it's hard to choose anything. I just want some basics, buying a lot of things would be a waste of money, since I don't know where they are sending me after I finish my training.

I take a long nap after finishing my chores, then I'm more than ready to go out and have some tequila.

Should I confess my sins?

Well then, I'll confess my sins.

I'm baffled by the fact that Adrik hasn't come looking for me, hasn't even deigned to send me a text message. This is when I wish I had some girlfriends, because that's who you turn to when dealing with man issues, right? I think back to my conversation with Roselynn and try to put some order in my head. Casper is my best friend but I'm not in the mood to talk to him, to be honest I am a little mad at him. He just dropped his bomb and left me alone to deal with the mess.

I think about Adrik again and the way I feel when he's close to me.

He makes me feel alive again, really alive. Adrik rekindled the flame within me that had lain dormant for so long, like the princess in the fairytale waiting for her handsome prince to ride in on his horse—in this case a metal steed—to wake her with that first kiss.

Love?

Do I know what love is? Does it really exist?

I wish I had one of those silly quizzes from a teen magazine that I used to love to buy when I was little so I could fill in all those little checkboxes to work out all this shit that's happening to me.

Did you feel attracted to him from the very first moment you saw him?

✓ Yes, but who wouldn't be?

Does he give you butterflies in the stomach?

✓ Yes, about the size of steroid fed pterodactyls.

Do you count the hours till you see him again?

✓ Too often, I'm afraid.

Does he make you laugh?

✓ Out loud. But he also makes me angry too, nobody makes my temper come out like him.

Do you have things in common?

✓ Deep down, I think so, we are two people looking at the same spot from different angles.

Shit. Did I even consider that?

I'm screwed.

Love.

Am I falling in love with Adrik Houston?

Love.

Damn four-letter word, I can understand why people fear it so much.

Come on, let's go get me some alcohol, I need it more than ever.

I bolster my confidence as much as I can with my outfit, without going overboard. My skinniest jeans, a loose blouse with a few embroidered beads, a black blazer, and high heels. This is me at my best, in an outfit that empowers me.

Fake it until you make it!

I hope to catch someone's eye to distract myself, for a while at least. I need get laid, to see if it'll ease the restlessness affecting my peace of mind.

I'm jumping out of the ride I ordered when I see Casper getting out of a luxury sedan. I take a deep breath to keep my bad mood at bay. I need tonight, I need this.

"Lexus?" I say as a greeting. "Wow, someone is being fancy here."

"A man does what he can, Didi," he replies, in his usual cheerful manner.

"Is there a girl you want to impress?"

"Something like that." He shrugs, without going into detail. I don't press him as we walk in together, I'm not in the mood to dig deeper.

The bar is just as I imagined, and it's very crowded. As soon as we enter, Anderson and Vargas spot us and signal for us to join them. Greg offers me the stool he was sitting on.

"You want a beer, Zanetti?" Vargas asks and I immediately accept.

It's very difficult to have a conversation in a place like this where the music is so loud, but my colleagues don't seem to care as they shout at each other, telling stupid jokes and laughing, it's just like being back at the academy.

"I'll be right back," Vargas announces. "This lion is going hunting. That girl over there, the one in the green dress, she is *hot*."

"Is that actually a dress she's wearing?" I ask, raising my eyebrows. "Wow, I think she left the skirt at home."

The dress is so short it barely covers her ass.

"And that's why she's perfect." He grins as he gets up. "Less fabric to remove."

We watch him walk over, and in less than five minutes he's already huddled in a corner with his conquest, having a much better night than us.

And for the record, it's not envy talking here.

"Right, Zanetti," Greg says, interrupting my thoughts. "What's this I hear about you with Commander Thunder?"

Casper frowns at the mention of Adrik, as do I.

I thought our little thing had remained behind closed doors.

"We only met up a few times but nothing happened between us." If he only knew…

"We're going in opposite directions, so we decided it was for best to leave it."

"That guy is the worst," Casper intervenes. "I sure hope they kick him out soon."

I hold my tongue, not wanting to give anything away. The less said on my part the better.

"Truth is, I like him," Greg responds. "I know a few sailors who've served under him and they say he's a good commander. Strict and demanding, but hey, we didn't enroll to be treated like princesses, right?"

"I've heard very different things," Casper states. "And I got it from a very good source."

"How about we change the subject?" I suggest. I came out tonight precisely to forget about Adrik, not to make him the topic of conversation.

"Does anyone want another drink?" Casper asks, searching for his wallet in his back pocket, and I silently thank him.

"Submarine!" Grace shouts.

"We want Zanetti! She has a round little butt and we want to see her in a bikini!" Thomson yells, as he serves the second round of submarines.

"In your dreams, bastard," I answer, knocking back my drink.

"Zanetti, you curse like a sailor," Vargas teases.

"That's because I am one, idiot."

"I would forget you're a woman, if you weren't so freaking hot," Thomson says as he walks toward me.

"You keep those hands away from me," I warn him. "Unless you want to lose one."

He lets out a laugh, raising his hands in surrender. Just what I need, my drunken colleagues making moves on me.

But I'm not interested, I need someone else. A big manly guy, with a badass face, and matching attitude. That's what I need, what I crave. Of course I'm not thinking about the one they call Thunder or the steel rod he keeps between his legs.

I look around, to see what else this place has to offer. At the end of the bar, there's a cute guy. I smile, he lifts his glass, and I do the same with what's left of mine.

"I'm just going to the bathroom. I'll be back in a minute, wait for me, and I'll get the next round," Casper says.

"Take it easy, Lieutenant. Maybe you should drink some water."

As soon as he leaves, I turn my attention back to the cute guy at the end of the bar and I mouth that I am going his way. He nods, pointing with his finger that he'll wait for me right where he is. I hurry through the crowd of people cramming the place.

Oh yeah. This girl is getting laid tonight.

Except that when I arrive, the cute guy seems to have vanished. Where the fuck did he go?

Or did I hallucinate him in the middle of my drunkenness?

I return to the spot where my friends are, as I keep looking around to see if I can spot the cute guy.

"Is everything okay?" Casper asks after a while.

"Sure, what makes you ask?"

"Just making sure you're having a good time."

I don't bother telling him that is not really the case, but then I feel something strange, a kind of electricity. As if someone were behind me, stroking my back with a feather, making me shudder. It's weird, but I just ignore whatever it is, putting it down to the alcohol I've consumed, deciding it's time to slow down a bit. My classmates might drink like Cossacks but I don't have as much tolerance. Even Casper, who doesn't usually drink that much, is quite tipsy.

"I'm going to look for a taxi to take us back to the base," I say to Casper when it's almost two in the morning and I'm more than ready to go.

"Don't you dare, I'm driving you back. I'm perfectly fine," he protests.

Nuh huh, he won't be driving me anywhere, he's wasted.

"Look at you, Casper. You aren't in the right state to drive. We're calling a ride and you are not going to argue about it."

We walk toward the exit and when I get to the sidewalk, I take off my shoes. Damn heels, they're killing me.

"Look," I exclaim, seeing a yellow car by the sidewalk. "There's a taxi."

"Didi," Casper replies. "I'm perfectly fine, I can drive, no problem."

He tries to impress me by walking in a straight line with his arms raised, but he fails miserably.

"If you want to risk killing yourself, you go right ahead, but I'm taking this cab."

"Didi, why are you being like this? Don't be so stubborn," he insists, taking my arm. "I can handle it, it's only a short drive to the base."

Dear Lord, how on earth did I get into this mess?

Casper takes me by the arm, begins to drag me over to where his car is parked.

"Let go of me!" I yell at him, because he is squeezing my arm too hard. "Casper, I'm not going anywhere with you!"

A few people are standing by watching, somewhat alarmed by this show on the sidewalk.

"Didi, take it easy. In less than ten minutes we'll be home, safe and sound."

Ten minutes? Does he want to fly or what?

"Casper, I told you to let go of me!" I demand, pulling my jacket sleeve from his grasp.

I'm about to hit his thick skull with my heel when I feel someone behind me.

"I suggest you let her go. Right the fuck now. We can do this the hard way, or the easy way," says a deep voice.

A voice that I know all too well.

I turn and there he is. Commander Thunder, ready to fight. And by his face, he's already on orange alert.

And the effect of alcohol suddenly vanishes.

One part of me is happy to see him, the other part wonders what the hell he's doing here.

"I told you to let her go," he warns Casper again, glaring at him, taking advantage of his superior height to stand menacingly over him, like a panther with its prey.

Casper reluctantly releases me, as he shrinks back, obviously as surprised as I am to see Adrik appear.

"Houston," my friend growls. "You aren't part of this celebration. This is a private party."

Adrik briefly looks at Casper before turning all his attention on me and, apparently, also his anger.

"What are you doing here?" I ask, when I manage to find my voice again.

"Looking out for you, of course. Why else would I be here?"

"She's here with me," Casper states. "I'm her best friend and I'm taking care of her."

Adrik doesn't even dignify that statement with a look. For him it is as if Casper were a fly, something that annoys him, but whose existence is not crucial. "You're not going anywhere with that fool, Jordania. He's wasted, he can hardly put one foot in front of the other."

"You think I don't know that? I'm not an idiot, Thunder."

"I'm not drunk," Casper protests. "Just a little tipsy."

"I'm going home in a taxi," I inform him, walking over to where they're parked, leaving them both to do as they please.

"Jordania, don't be stubborn," Adrik says, his voice sounding like a warning, a threat. "Are you coming with me or do I have to throw you over my shoulder?"

Oh?

"You wouldn't dare."

I look at him and he raises an eyebrow, ready to pick up the gauntlet I just threw down.

"Didi, I've got the car keys," Casper calls over to me, as if it were a big deal.

Adrik completely ignores him.

"Why are you so angry?" I ask. "This has nothing to do with you."

What is his problem?

"I told you I didn't want you going out with those morons to get drunk, because I knew exactly how things would turn out. What would have happened if I hadn't come looking for you? How the hell would you have returned to the base?"

"I was about to get a taxi, not that it's any of your business, idiot," I snap as he tries to take my hand.

"You will always be my business, and apparently my headache."

"I don't want to be anything to you, not your pain or anything."

Liar! A little voice shouts from the back of my conscience. *Damn, why don't you shut the fuck up, stupid conscience?*

Casper reaches for my hand and tries to pull me toward him with the little strength he has in his intoxicated state.

But Adrik blocks him, then pushes him away onto a nearby car.

They are about to hit each other and it's clear that Casper will not come out of this well since Commander Thunder is in full destructive mode.

"Please, just go. I have this situation under control." I give it one last try.

"Jordania, it's too late for games."

"Who are you to talk?" I challenge. "You think I'm the one playing games now? Well, I'm not the one who walked out of my condo last time."

"You're playing a game you won't be able to finish, beautiful."

"Just leave me alone!" I yell again.

"Enough. We're leaving, this show is over," he says quietly, but firmly. "This is not the time or place to talk about our outstanding issues."

"Didi..." I hear Casper groaning, noticing that he's about to fall and faceplant into the concrete sidewalk.

"I have to put Casper in a taxi, I can't let him drive," I say. That's a good reason to take a break, Adrik can't be *that* stubborn.

But as always, he has to be a man of action and take control.

He goes to the first taxi driver he finds and, despite his protests, gets Casper into the vehicle.

"My car? Where is my car?" I hear Casper whining. "I can't leave my new car parked in the street."

"He can come back tomorrow to pick it up," he says to me. Of course for the magnificent Adrik Houston, Casper, it's not an issue, Casper is just a rock on his path that he can kick and keep walking.

I give in and the tension caused by my anger goes away. Now something else is floating in the air between us. Adrik lifts me up in his arms and walks away with me, as if I was weightless.

"This isn't necessary, I can walk," I say quietly, not feeling like arguing anymore, I'm just sleepy, very sleepy, damn alcohol. Where is my sassiness when I need it? "And I'm not going with you on that hell horse you own."

There it is, that sounds like me.

"Why are you walking barefoot?" he murmurs. "I told you I would take care of you, because *I care about you*. I like you, Jordania, maybe too much for my own sanity."

I thought we were talking about him carrying me in his arms, but suddenly I get the idea that we've fallen into very deep waters.

We arrived at a dark gray truck with heavily tinted windows.

"Hold on to me," he orders, and for once I don't feel like arguing so I just comply, wanting to bury my nose into his neck, to feel close to him again, to get drunk on his cologne, his essence that I've missed so much.

Adrik opens the car door and settles me in the seat, making sure I'm secured with my seat belt before he jogs around to the driver's side.

"Why did you come, Adrik?" I ask, as he starts the engine.

"Don't you know?" He leans toward me, his body is so warm and I've missed him so freaking much.

The engine is running, but we haven't moved from the parking spot.

"No, not really. I have my suspicions, but I can't be sure." I want him to spell it out for me.

"Why are you making this so difficult?"

I shrug. "Just because."

"Look, you little brat, I just need you to be safe. So if you want to escape and let off steam, then get drunk with *me*."

His lips touch mine, my mouth opens to welcome him and I'm done for.

Over and out.

Rule # 12: When talking about seduction, turn fear into trust, anticipation into desire, and fantasy into reality.

Chapter TWELVE

How good it feels to wake up wrapped in a protective, warm hug. Slowly I open my eyes to find I'm in a room that isn't mine. This must be Adrik's room and I'm in his bed.

Fortunately, the blinds are closed, so the light doesn't bother me and thankfully my head isn't pounding either.

I close my eyes again, remembering everything that happened last night. Arguing with Casper at the bar. Adrik carrying me in his arms to his truck. A kiss, then falling asleep.

Damn Sandman, picking the worst time to visit me.

I also remember returning to the building. Being carried in his arms. His strength, his warmth, his strong chest. The kisses that he scattered over my skin as I took off my clothes.

But from that moment on, my mind is blank.

I wanted to be with Adrik so much, I've craved it, fantasized about it, and now I don't have a clue what happened.

Fuck my luck.

At this point I can only guess how good it might have been.

I can only imagine how it felt to have him moving inside me, invading me, making me his.

I roll over and find him still sleeping on his back. The sheet only covering him from his waist down gives me the chance to get lost watching him.

Awake, he's so imposing and cocky, but now completely relaxed, he is the most handsome man I have ever seen. Stubble covers his chin, casting a soft shadow over his features. I look closely at the fine wrinkles he has here and there, that instead of diminishing his appeal, they give him character. And, that, without a doubt, is his greatest attribute.

He's so strong and I feel safe with him. For a woman who has spent her life keeping her walls up, it feels nice to let them down and relax a little.

In this moment, I'm just the simple girl at the waterfall having fun under the sun.

My fingers itch to touch him, to trace paths on his skin, and get lost in them.

But there is something I must do first.

I really need the bathroom, so thankfully it's the first door I find as I get out of bed, realizing that I'm not naked. I'm still in my underwear, meaning Adrik didn't take advantage of my inebriated state.

A sense of relief sweeps over me, along with another feeling that I don't want to examine too closely as it expands on my chest.

"I'm an honest man, and I will always tell you the truth," I recall him telling me at my apartment. Maybe it's time to start believing he really doesn't lie.

What else have I been wrong about?

Casper's stories?

Adrik's bedroom is bigger than mine and although it's fully furnished, for some reason it gives me the impression it's not really his taste, the upholstered bed frame doesn't have *my* Commander's vibes.

I feel like an intruder looking in the drawers of the bathroom for a brand new toothbrush, but thankfully everything is so neat and organized that I quickly find one. There's no clutter, just the basic necessities and some good quality toiletries.

Thank God the man owns a comb, so I can tame the rat's nest on my head.

Five minutes later, somewhat more composed, I'm ready to go back to bed, and into his arms.

"I'm surprised you're up so early," he comments when he sees me enter the room.

I'm not a self-conscious woman, nakedness doesn't bother me. My body may have its defects but I have learned to love them. However, with his burning gaze running over my skin, I feel like a shy teenager again.

"Seems you were a perfect gentleman last night," I whisper as his eyes roaming over me practically set me on fire.

"I told you before, I'm not Prince Charming, and I'm certainly not a gentleman either."

My eyes travel over his smooth chest, his small brown nipples, and his muscled arms marked with veins.

"Are you hungry?" I ask, trying to cool things and create some space between us.

Why am I so nervous?

The sensible thing is to have a calm conversation before anything happens. Because I'm as sure as my name is Jordania Marie Zanetti that today is going to be the day we step over the line.

"I'm hungry for *you*," he replies with a smirk. "I could eat you for breakfast."

"Then do it, big bad wolf."

The sheet flies off as Adrik gets out of bed and picks me up in his arms. With the white bedroom wall behind me, I arch my body to offer myself to him.

Here, with his mouth running over my curves, I feel wanted, feminine, free.

Perfect.

His.

All too soon I'll have to become myself again, but for now I just want to fly into his arms, get away, escape to that place where I know he can take me. Only him.

His lips keep heading down my body, until, with my legs over his arms, he lifts me up, making his intentions clear.

Crystal clear.

When his tongue touches my core, I cry out his name, telling him that I want him, that I need more. I scream because it overwhelms me and drives me crazy.

Because he sets me on fire and burns me.

He continues to feed on my body, devouring my essence, it's so intense it's almost painful. I reach the edge of the abyss and there is no option but to give in to his demands and his direct orders. The pressure builds, my body burns, and as I reach my release, I dig my nails deep into his shoulders as I let go.

My whole body shudders, my knees shake as Adrik lowers me to the floor, but before I can worry about standing, he presses me back against the wall, taking my face in his hands to stare at me.

His eyes tell me everything I want to know.

Adrik caresses my face with a gentleness that overwhelms me, outlining the line of my eyebrows, my cheeks, until he focuses his attention on my parted lips.

"I want to do so many things to you," he murmurs.

"Then why are you wasting precious time, Commander Thunder?"

Tangling his fingers in the thick strands of my messy hair, he takes my mouth with his, dipping inside, inviting my tongue to dance with his as he holds me tightly against him.

Surrounding him with my arms I cling to him, devouring him, craving him as I rub my body against his, against the hardness still concealed in his tight shorts. My fingers sink into his shoulders as he grips my ass in his big hands. Somehow, I end up on my back on the bed, while he quickly gets rid of his boxers and slips between my thighs, leaning over me.

Then slowly, slowly yet decisively, his body finally enters mine.

And fuck, it feels so good.

I forget the before and after, focusing only on the here and now. This is us. The feeling of pleasure increases with each thrust, making me his, as he becomes mine.

"That's it," he growls in my ear. "I need you to come again, this time around me."

His body dominates mine with the mastery of someone who knows how to control his strength, loving me slowly, inch by inch. I'm needy, I want it all. I squeeze his ass to pull him deeper into me, causing him to growl before he laughs and gives me what I need.

"This is paradise," he groans. "I want to die right here between your legs."

"Adrik," I cry out, and with what strength I have left I claw at his back, leaving my mark on him, my breath lost in the ether of my surrender.

His lips touch me, his wet tongue and his teeth playing with my breasts, making me groan, as my muscles clench and my release bursts through me.

Adrik doesn't cease in his quest for ecstasy, making me feel like a rag doll, carried away by the fire that he continues to stoke, preventing me from thinking.

I feel him everywhere, his skin is confused with mine and the fire consumes me.

"Jordania," he cries out as he finally lets himself go over the edge to his climax.

As we both come down, he rolls us over on the sheets, without letting me go, taking me with him.

"That was something else, Jordania, just as I knew it would be. There is no one else in the world like you," he whispers, kissing my forehead.

He's so intense that the bubble bursts, bringing me back from the land of fantasy, back to reality.

"Adrik," I sigh. "What happens now?"

"We'll have breakfast and then we'll come back to bed," he replies. "I don't know about you, but I'm not done yet. I want more."

I reprimand him with a gentle slap on the chest.

"Don't be so obtuse. You know what I mean."

"Yeah, I know," he acknowledges, putting his head back on the pillow as he covers his eyes with his arm.

"So, what are we going to do?"

"Is there a protocol for this?" he asks without looking at me. "I know what I want, but what do your damn rules say?"

"I need more time to get my head around things," I admit with a sad chuckle. I want to bury myself away and hide. "Because I'm very aware that a man like you could be the end of me."

He moves on top of me, to look me in the eye.

"You can't stop worrying, right?" I nod my head and he continues. "Jordania, just let things develop at their own pace. Let's do what normal couples do, let's go out to dinner, to the movies, do whatever shit we feel like doing. Let's get to know each other, see where this takes us."

My courage has left me. I feel completely open and vulnerable, helpless.

"Adrik, this is too much, *you are* too much."

"The only thing that's too much here is the fear you have," he says. "Stop overanalyzing things, let's just enjoy ourselves, life is too short."

"I can't help it," I admit, because it's the truth. "It's just the way I am."

"Then I'll settle for kiss me for now," he orders. "We'll work on the rest later."

"You're so bossy," I reply, pretending to be upset.

I don't fool him for a second.

"I'm not bossy, in bed I am the boss."

"So freaking humble, *sir.*" I draw out this last word and he gives me a spank on the butt.

"I thought you would be used to it by now."

I do what he orders and I'm pleasantly rewarded.

One. Two. Three times.

"You know there are going to have to be some rules, right?" I tell him later, when we have finally get out of bed and are in his kitchen. He's preparing spinach and cheese omelets for breakfast.

I'm sitting at his breakfast bar sipping coffee and enjoying the view. It's great—he's doing all the cooking while I'm just eating and piling on the pounds.

Every time he moves his back muscles stretch, and the inked lines on his shoulder have me salivating for more than food.

Dang, I'm going to be sore tomorrow and I don't give a fuck about it.

"You do surprise me," he chuckles as he rolls his eyes at me.

"Save the sarcasm, Thunder," I retort. "It's the way I do things, so you're going to have to deal with it."

As I stretch up over the counter to get some glasses from the shelf above, he traps me there, forcing me to look at him.

"What if we create new rules? Adapt them, make them work for both of us."

"This is all happening so fast, Houston, and there are so many problems, thousands of them in fact."

"The main problem is that you still don't trust me," he says, and he is absolutely right.

He reached the heart of the matter.

"Well, if you had taken the time to explain a few things, maybe I'd find it easier to put my trust in you."

"Then just ask me," he states. "Talk to me, tell me what the hell it is you want from me."

"For starters, I want you to take it easy, be more patient with me, not try and rush things."

"Jordania, believe me," he says, "I'm trying my hardest to bide my time and be patient with you. Otherwise, I would've bitten your head off a long time ago, because you can be so fucking stubborn when you put your mind to it."

"Ok, just remember about being patient and that'll be a good start." Now I think it best to steer this conversation back in a more general direction. "So, tell me why your apartment is already furnished, when you told me you arrived shortly after me."

"Being a senior officer has its benefits." He grins. "The officer who lived here before left everything behind. From the couple items in the dresser, I think it was female."

As he talks, he turns to give me his full attention, and I feel we're making progress. We're having a normal conversation. Maybe getting to know him won't be that hard.

"Then why were we at my place, sitting on my uncomfortable barstools?"

"If you recall, I did invite you here," he points out. "And I told you about the magnificent view. Speaking of which, we should have dinner on the balcony this evening to admire the sunset."

A warm rush floods through me at the thought of us sharing a meal and enjoying the view together, just like our first date in Hawaii.

"You have a deal." I smile.

He serves the omelets and sits beside me, kissing my shoulder covered by one of his Navy t-shirts.

"You look so beautiful wearing my clothes. I'd love to see you in my camo."

Thinking about it gives me chills, having his last name on my chest.

Stop it, you crazy freak. It's just the beginning, don't get ahead of yourself.

"Why do they really call you Commander Thunder? Come on, I want the whole story," I demand and he laughs.

"You're really curious about it, right?"

"Sure," I answer, raising my eyebrows. "Tell me the truth."

"You'll never get anything other than the whole truth from me."

"So tell me then," I insist.

"Fine, Thunder isn't just a nickname, it's my call sign. Zephyr Herrera, one of my lieutenants and also my friend, came up with the idea," he laughs, making me smile. "And for the record, it has nothing to do with women."

"What happened?"

"Once, Zeph organized a trip to Baja, to a beautiful place called Cerritos. We were exhausted after a long tour, and all we wanted was to relax and surf, but things didn't go as planned. Zephyr made a mess of the reservations and they canceled the lodging, the food we'd taken was mysteriously spoiled, everything was turning into a disaster. To top it all off, we didn't even get to surf, because there were no waves, the sea was calm for three days in a row."

"What does that have to do with thunder?"

He laughs again.

"Well, one night when we were drunk, I began to conjure, Sergeant Dan style. Then the next day an epic storm came, complete with thunder…"

"And so ever since then you've been Commander Thunder," I whisper and he responds with a shrug.

"I wasn't a commander at the time, but yes. Is the interrogation over?" he asks after a few minutes of silence. "Can we have breakfast and then dessert?"

"Yes, let's eat because I'm starving. However, this conversation isn't over yet, not by a long shot."

"God, have mercy on me."

"Don't blaspheme," I scold.

"I'm not, I'm being serious, Jordania," he replies. "Let's see, when are you going out with me?"

Let the battle begin!

At least for now.

But before we can continue, his cell phone goes off, and he picks it up from the countertop immediately.

"I have to take this, sorry."

When he hears the voice on the other end of the line, his face morphs completely, his brows furrow, and his jaw clenches.

"How long ago?" he asks and then silence. "No, don't let him inside the house, I'm on my way."

Rule # 13: Don't ask for something you aren't willing to share.

Chapter THIRTEEN

"What's happening?" I ask as soon he ends the call.

He closes his eyes and takes a deep breath before answering. "My father is at my grandparent's home. He's making a scene and upsetting my grandma. To top it all off today's one of her bad days and she doesn't remember what happened the last time he made an appearance."

Fuck, fuck, fuck. This is heavy shit.

"I'm sorry, baby," he says before giving me another kiss on the shoulder. "I gotta go."

We both stand, and before I can stop myself, the words pop out of my mouth. "I'm going with you."

Adrik stops in his tracks and stares at me.

"Are you sure you want to get involved in this?"

Not really, but I know I want to be there to support him.

"Sure." I shrug nonchalantly.

He thinks about it for a couple seconds. "Okay. I need to take a quick shower, then we'll go to your apartment so you can get ready. I'll be back in few minutes. You stay here."

Huh? Why is he insisting I stay in his kitchen?

"Don't be silly, it'll be quicker if we shower together, then head back to my place to get my clothes."

I have to bite my lip to stop myself from laughing at the face he pulls.

"If you get in that shower with me, Jordania, we would never leave."

I roll my eyes at him.

"Don't be ridiculous, I'm sure you can exert a little self-control. We'll both quickly shower here, then we can be on our way." I walk toward the bathroom, patting him on the shoulder as I pass.

"You'll pay for this," he groans, shaking his head as he follows me.

Truthfully, keeping our hands off each other is easier said than done, but I guess Adrik's worry about his grandmother takes over and forces him to behave.

We run to my apartment and while he makes a call, I look for something to wear.

We're going on the bike, which means jeans, a leather jacket, sneakers, and a ponytail to control my hair.

"Thanks, Herrera," I hear him say from the living room. My bedroom door is open and I'm quickly tying my sneakers. "I'm taking Jordania with me." Another pause. "Yes, no worries, I'll call you later if I need to, although I hope that won't be necessary."

I hear him opening the sliding glass door to the small balcony, and I find him out there, lost in his thoughts.

"Ready to go. You OK?"

My hand slides up his back and along his shoulder until it rests on the back of his strong neck, softly caressing him.

He stands there for a minute, enjoying my touch, then straightens his back, and takes my hand.

"We need to get going." He hands me a black helmet.

This isn't the same bike we rode in Kauai. If that one was a hell horse, this is like one of horses of the Apocalypse. It's black, enormous, yet beautiful.

"My butt won't fit on that tiny seat, Adrik." I frown as he secures my helmet.

"Your pretty little ass will be just fine. Don't worry, I'll be sure to take care of any discomfort later." He winks and climbs on the bike.

I climb on behind him, and soon enough we're heading away from the complex on freeway 15 North. At first I lock my arms around Adrik's waist, but after a couple of minutes, he takes my hands and pulls me closer, leaving them resting on his hard chest.

Fine by me.

Some would say this is an adventure. Seeing the city from another perspective, while I'm in my own happy little bubble, holding on tightly to this enigma of a man, that I'm still trying to figure out.

I want him to be mine.

I'm not looking for a perfect man, I just want someone who'll accept me for who I am, with all my quirkiness, yet still be strong enough not to be a doormat.

I'm not sure if Adrik is the one, but I think I'm ready to take a risk.

I want to see where life leads us.

Life isn't about the destination, it's about the ride. And right here, right now, I'm enjoying it very much.

In less than twenty-five minutes, Adrik slows down to take the exit and drives us to a cul-de-sac with cute one-story ranch style houses with manicured front yards.

He parks in a driveway behind an old silver Volvo and takes his helmet off.

As we are getting off the bike, I see an older version of Adrik walk toward us. The man I assume is his father is as tall as Adrik is, a bit thinner, with hair like salt and pepper, and handsome as a devil. Beauty is in their genes, that's a fact.

"What the hell are you doing here?" Adrik demands, as he takes a few steps in front of me shielding my body, almost as if we're on a battlefield.

"Well, look at you, my son," the man replies, a smirk pulling up on his lips.

"You're nothing to me, I'm not your son. The only father I've ever known is inside that house, dealing with his sick wife."

"And I came to see them, to visit for a while."

"The fuck you are." Adrik's back tenses as he speaks to his father, and I can tell he's furious.

"I don't see what the problem is. Isn't it the duty of a good son to take care of his elderly parents?"

Adrik laughs sourly.

"It's too late for that. Just leave, go, do whatever it was you were doing before. We don't need you here."

I try my best to let him know I'm here for him, to offer some comfort in what is clearly a shitty situation. I slip my hand onto his back, just below his biker jacket, touching his warm skin through the thin fabric of his t-shirt.

He takes a step back, leaning into my touch.

It's reassuring. For the both of us.

It makes me feel useful even though I don't know how to deal with this.

"I just want to be here with all of you," his father pleads. "You're the only family I have."

Those words break my heart, and make me feel like crying. I don't know what I'd do if I were in Adrik's place, if my father had left me as a small child, the way his father did.

But Adrik isn't about to give in. He has his sword held high, ready to fight, and kill if necessary. He frowns, his dark sunglasses concealing his eyes.

"I have no idea why you felt the need to come, but there's no place for you here. Just tell me how much you want this time and then you can go fuck yourself."

"Son, it's not about money."

"With you it's always about money. You don't give a shit about us, you're not interested in anyone but yourself," Adrik spits out. "I have a couple of thousand with me, just take it then crawl back to the hole you came from."

"You're wrong. This time it really isn't about money," the man insists before turning and walking away.

"Always has been before, so I don't see why it'd be any different *this time*," Adrik states firmly.

"And for the record," his father says stopping, but without turning around, "I don't expect you to understand, but I did what I thought was best for *you*. That's why I brought you here, that's why I left you with them." And then he walks away.

Adrik jerks back as if something heavy just hit him. If those words have an impact on me, I can't even imagine what they mean to him.

Being abandoned. Discarded. Growing up thinking you'd been rejected for some reason.

After a moment, he pulls on my hand to bring me closer to him and hug the hell out of me until I can barely breathe. Thank God my ribs are strong since he's holding me hard enough to crack one.

He kisses my head before taking my hand again and leading me to the house.

Before we reach the door, it swings open and an elderly man with a walker appears. This time Adrik smiles, and the man smiles back. Without a shadow of a doubt, this is his grandfather. As I said before, good looks run in their genes.

"I don't know what to do," the man says after Adrik hugs and kisses him. "You know how upset your Nana gets when she sees him."

Adrik pats his grandpa's arm and turns to me.

"Papa, this is my girl, Jordania Zanetti," he says, smiling proudly and standing tall. "Baby, this is Adair Houston, my grandfather."

"Nice to meet you, Mr. Houston." I hold my hand out to him.

"You can call me Papa," he says, hugging me. "Come with me. But first I need to know how this silly boy tricked you into coming here with him."

Adrik rolls his eyes and that makes me smile again. This light banter, the love that flows between them is undeniable.

I'm happy to be here to witness it.

"You sure caught a pretty one." Adrik's grandfather winks as he offers me his arm, and I slip my hand around his elbow while we walk inside. "I taught you well. After all, I managed to get the prettiest girl to marry me all those years ago."

"Where is Nana?" Adrik asks, looking around as we stand in the kitchen. The house is warm and cozy, nothing too fancy, but not too shabby or rundown either, it's clean, and charming.

"The nurse gave her a mild sedative which put her to sleep, but hopefully she wakes up before you leave. You know how much she misses you."

"Sure thing," Adrik replies, looking toward the hall.

"Coffee?" Adair asks, walking over to the coffeepot.

"Latté, for you, baby?" Adrik asks me with a smile and my heart melts. Yup, I'm in serious trouble.

Three hours later, we're sitting around an iron table on the patio, sipping iced tea, and laughing while Adair tells me Adrik's childhood stories. He brought out a photo album and is proudly showing me every milestone.

"He came to us as a newborn, his father brought him here directly from the hospital. He was a big baby with a good set of lungs, he kept us awake for weeks before he settled. But Luana, my wife, was on cloud nine, and I was too tired to argue with her."

"Hey, I'm listening, Papa!" Adrik pretends to be upset.

Adair looks at Adrik with so much love in his eyes. A lump fills my throat as I think about Adrik's father's words, why he brought him here, to his parents' home.

Sometimes, the best thing you can do for someone you love is to give them up, no matter how hard it is, especially if you are not able to give them what they need.

Because of that, in my book, Adrik's father isn't so bad. Don't misunderstand me, I can't stand the man. But I agree with him, and I can see that maybe he did what he thought was best for his child.

He gave him a secure, loving home.

It's almost four in the afternoon when we leave Adrik's family home. I didn't get the chance to meet his Nana, but Adair makes me promise to come back soon.

"We'll be waiting to see you on Thanksgiving," he said as we leave. "Take good care of my boy."

"Papa…" Adrik protests.

But smiling I reply, "I will. See you soon, Papa."

"Don't let this one go, boy."

In the end, Adrik just growls and takes my hand to lead me back to his bike.

On the way back to the base, Adrik takes a different road, driving east, I think. My theory is confirmed once we enter a beachside parking lot.

It isn't that crowded, the breeze is soft but chilly, and the scenery is amazing.

"Where are we?"

"This is the Oceanside Pier," he says. "I like this place very much, and I figured you'd be hungry after having your ear chewed off by my Papa with all his stories. There's a restaurant at the end of the pier where they serve great burgers along with a great view."

"And fries too, right?"

"And fries too."

He laughs, as if all the things troubling him have disappeared.

"Let's take a walk."

Hand in hand we climb up the stairs to the long wooden platform and then amble along past all the people here—some are fishing, others just enjoying the scenery. Kids are running around a man with an enormous bubble maker, and in the sea, a few surfers are catching the waves.

This feels so normal, as if this was meant to be. It feels so easy being here with him, as if our relationship has taken a huge step forward since I met his family, maybe only part of it, but still.

At the restaurant the hostess informs us we'll have to wait for a table, as the place is filled to the brim, so we have time to go for a walk and talk.

"Are you ready to run yet?" he asks. He's standing behind me, my back against his chest. I'm sandwiched between him and the wooden rail facing the ocean.

"Oh, I get it now," I say, smiling. "This was all just a trick to spook me so you could be free again."

He takes a deep breath, and we're so close I can feel everything, even his heart beating against my body.

"Guess it was kind of a reality check," he admits. "I was trying to impress you and then bam, it all went to shit. So now is your chance, Jordania, just say you don't want to be with me, I completely understand with all my issues…"

"What if I do want to be with you?"

We can't have this conversation looking out to sea, I need to look into his eyes, to read him.

"A few days ago, you said you didn't want to change me, Adrik. So, if you can accept me with all my faults, then surely I should do the same for you?"

"Jordania, I want to really get to know you, the real you, to learn how to love you. You, with your fire and water, like on the island. With all of your truths, with all of your quirks. I'm all in, I'm not interested in half measures—I want all of you—the totality of you. I want to hold you whenever you need me to. I want to take you out on dates. I want to lay with you in my bed every single day, every single night."

He's totally making me cry. I'm trembling. My heart is melting. Luckily, I have thick wooden planks beneath me as my stupid legs are refusing to cooperate.

"You're stubborn and fierce, and so fucking genuine. I don't want to put boundaries around you, I want you to fly, to take me with you. I want to *know* you, the real you. The free you. Shine your light on me, drown me in your love, get to know me as well as you know yourself, devour my soul with your divinity… I want you and I want to be as one with you. Allow yourself to depend on me. Stop playing games, because when you're with me, you don't need to put on a front, you don't have to be the woman of steel, you don't need to be afraid of appearing weak. I want everything, I want us to reach into infinity, I want to reach forever with you."

Two big fat tears are wetting my cheeks, I can't help it. I really can't. I want to reach forever with him too, I want to get lost in those smoky eyes that are now fixed on me.

He's barely touching me, yet I can feel him everywhere.

Imprinting my heart with his words.

Staining my soul with his colors.

Joy fills my heart and runs through my veins. He's like one of those waves the surfers are waiting to ride, but instead of catching, it drags me to the bottom of the ocean.

We aren't a perfect match. We're both strong, we're both stubborn, and determined to get our way.

This relationship won't be easy.

But.

Nothing worth having ever comes easy.

We are like a force of nature about to collide.

Thunder and lightning.

Powerful.

Striking.

Eternal.

Our lips meet and I have so much to give him with this kiss, more than words can say, so much happiness, it's threatening to make me explode.

And then someone calls his name.

"Houston! Table for two." Shit, all I want is go back to the base, to his bed, but a meal with a view awaits us.

This restaurant has retro vibes, with a jukebox in the corner, and waiters dressed in white uniforms with cute aprons and hats.

But nothing is more beautiful than the view.

My man sits opposite of me in a red vinyl covered booth, with a big window to the side, where we can see the sun setting on the horizon coloring the blue sea and the sky.

I'm an avocado lover, so I can't resist ordering some on my burger, while Adrik orders one with tons of cheese and mushrooms.

We're sipping our soft drinks, when a man with some of those long thin balloons approaches us, leans against the booth, and whispers to Adrik.

He laughs when Adrik explains something in low voice, their eyes sparkling with mischief.

"Gotcha!" the man says to Adrik. "I'll be back in a few…" Then runs off to God knows where.

"What are you up to, *Commander?*" I emphasize the last word, hoping he catches my drift.

And of course he does.

"I'm planning to feed you, because you're going to need plenty of energy for when we arrive back at my place. I'm planning to have my way with you all night long."

Check, please!

Adrik smirks, but this time he isn't looking at me, but at something *behind* me.

He nods at the same time I hear a voice announcing, "Voila!"

And then he puts something on my head.

What the…

"Here is my pineapple. Crown and all."

"What?"

I remove the thing from my head while Adrik pays the balloon artist, and then I smile, remembering what he said to me in Kauai, which seems eons ago.

I can't believe we're here, sharing a meal as a real couple.

Because we're giving this, us, a chance.

A chance with Commander Thunder. Oh my, I think I lost my freaking mind.

And I don't have a single regret.

"Please don't tell me you wear those scraps of lace under your uniform every day," he comments later in my bedroom. I'm packing a bag to spend the next few days in his apartment.

"Okay, I won't," I reply, forcing my attention back to putting the folded clothes in the suitcase.

"Next time I'll order that guy to make you sexy angel's wings," he says, playing with the balloon crown.

"Don't you dare." I point at him, thinking that's too much information for the balloon man. My secrets should remain behind closed doors, just between us.

"You and that lingerie you love so much will be the end of me," he declares.

"I'm a sailor, but I'm also a woman. And this woman loves pretty things, like perfume and lace. I'm fire and water, like you said."

He's on my bed, leaning back on the headboard—sans jacket, just a cotton t-shirt stretching across his wide chest—while watching my every move like a hawk, his patience hanging by a thread.

Adrik is like a cat, one second he's on the bed, the next he's stretched over me, his big hands grabbing my wrists, and placing them on either side of my head.

"You need to be very quiet," he murmurs, as his mouth travels south.

"And why is that?"

"Because we haven't made it to my place yet. You have neighbors and these walls are pretty thin."

"Oh yeah?"

"A man can only take so much, baby, and you've been tempting me all day long. Enough is enough." My t-shirt flies off and lands on the floor.

Next, he takes care of the zipper on my jeans.

"What if I want to be in control this time? Haven't you heard about woman on top, *sir?*"

He looks down at me, his face serious, then flips us onto the bed, taking me with him.

"Come and sit on my face, then I'll give you my very own version of having a woman on top."

Straddling his torso until my pussy is right over his face, my hips grind while his hands go up my body, right to my lace covered tits, squeezing and playing with both nipples, creating magic. The things this man can do with that tongue...

I'm about to call him sir, which is ridiculous, but thinking about it is so freaking hot.

I'm about to explode.

"Not yet," he orders.

Adrik is stretched out on his back, my body over his, as he holds my hands behind my back and starts kissing me, running his wicked tongue over my lips and into my mouth, letting me taste myself.

I'm a volcano... fire and water...

He releases my hands, so they can wander freely over his body, going down to his abs, then stroking his cock, loving how big and hard he feels.

He's demanding, and giving.

I want to feel him moving inside me.

But Adrik hasn't finished with his torture. The man has an agenda of his own as he slides his cock between my legs and over my pussy, teasing me, rubbing the entire length of his shaft down my clit, until I'm soaking wet for him.

What is he doing to me?

Then he slides his cock deep into me—it hurts in the most delicious way—bottoming out as he stretches me to the limit, letting me feel his throbbing cock deep inside me, while his mouth gets to work on my nipples, biting them as he starts fucking me faster and faster, deeper and deeper.

He's casting a powerful spell over me, and I can't deny the pleasure he's giving me.

"Scream my name," he orders.

And I do.

Because I'm a good girl.

For him, anyway.

Right?

Rule # 14: Sometimes, the small things can make a big difference.

Chapter FOURTEEN

Time seems to have grown wings, as it is flying by so quickly.

Five weeks ago I was all grumpy about my transfer and now I couldn't imagine being in any other city.

This place is amazing, and not just the base. The entire city is awesome, there is so much to explore, so many places to go, and so much beauty to enjoy.

There is just one thing raining on my parade and he's standing in front of me.

Casper has turned up at my apartment, and is watching me pack some of my stuff that I'm taking to Adrik's. I found my old friend waiting by my door when I got back from work.

"I want you to know that I'm not happy with your decision, Didi," Casper declares, as he watches me pick out some things from one of my drawers, folding t-shirts, and putting them on the bed.

Every day I'm spending less time here and more time in Adrik's apartment. Between the lack of furniture and his demands, we've ended up migrating from the sixth to the top floor. Plus I have to admit the view from his balcony is much more beautiful.

"It's not about you, Casper," I reply irritably. I know he doesn't like Adrik, but still, it's none of his business. "It's not about what you want. This is my life and it's my choice, not yours."

Casper walks around the bedroom, looking at the furniture, almost as if he were searching for something.

Gah, now I'm imagining things. I look up at the white painted ceiling, begging for patience, or mercy at least. I'm about to strangle my friend.

"I know, Didi, but as your best friend, I have to tell you that I'm worried," he insists. "Houston is not the man for you. I just hope you don't realize that when it's too late."

"It's a risk I've decided to take," I say, lifting my chin stubbornly.

If we don't change the subject, I'm going to throw him out the window. I'm getting fed up with Casper. Sure, he has been a loyal friend for a long time, and I'm grateful that he has always been there for me, but even gratitude has its limits.

"Didi, you're playing with fire."

I know this, but it's one of the things I love about Adrik. However, I bite my tongue and don't say anything.

"What about all the gossip your behavior is causing around the base? Aren't you concerned about it affecting your career as a future commander? This gossip is bound to reach your father's ears, it's only a matter of time."

Adrik and I came to an agreement, deciding that we weren't going to keep our relationship secret, but that it still isn't anybody's business, but ours.

We're both single, with no commitments, so why shouldn't we see each other?

"Gossip is just that, Casper. Gossip," I say firmly. "I'm not going to allow myself to be paralyzed with fear, worrying about what others say about me. As long as I'm happy with what I'm doing and how I act, then why should the rest of the world give a damn?"

"And are you happy?" he asks seriously.

Am I happy? I think about it for a moment, then look into his eyes, before finally answering.

"Yes, I truly am." I smile. "For the first time in a long time, I feel really happy."

"Well, I just hope your happiness lasts," he says bitterly. "But I won't be holding my breath."

Why is this such an issue for him?

The conversation I had with Roselynn, the girl at the bakery, comes to mind and hits me like a ton of bricks.

He's jealous, and he's manipulating you.

I don't know if that's true, but right now Casper is certainly annoying me, and that's never a good thing.

I close my bag and turn to look at him. Casper is leaning on the dresser with his arms crossed in front of his chest, looking like a father ready to give his kid *the lecture*.

Sorry, but the father role is already taken.

"What is it that you want from me?" I ask, hoping he'll get to the point or leave me alone.

"I want you to do the right thing, Didi. Why are you being so blind?"

Yes, I'm completely blind right now, because all I see is red.

"Why are you doing this, Casper? You're going to lose me as a friend if you carry on like this."

"He's changed you, and not for the better. You're not the friend I used to know, Jordania," he replies, his face flushed, his fists clenched tightly by his side.

I put my suitcase down on the floor, more than ready to end this conversation and get the hell out of here.

"I've always been your friend, it's just a shame that's not enough for you."

"I want my old friend back. I don't know you anymore."

"I'm beginning to think I never really knew you at all."

"That's not true, Didi. You're my soul mate and we were meant to end up together, until Houston turned your head."

What the heck?

"If you were truly my friend, you'd be happy for me. Can't you see that?"

He stares at me again, looking ready to burst.

"I'm sorry, but I can't take this anymore. I can't stand seeing you act this way."

As I walk to the bedroom door, I turn to look back at him. "This is my life and I'm not changing how I act, so you can just fuck off, Casper."

I close the door of the apartment with a heavy heart, as I leave a huge part of my past in there, along with our friendship.

"I have here the list of vessels that have been allocated to each of you. However, as we've decided to carry out some extra field exercises first, you'll have to continue working theoretically for now," our instructor informs us in his harsh authoritarian voice. Some days he's so demanding that I almost pity us. There are six destroyers—like us, they are being thoroughly tested—and by the time we've completed the next cycle, we'll be more than ready to head out to sea. "You better be prepared, I'm warning you now, and this isn't a vacation."

Yup, this is great news. We have to learn every single detail about the vessels and their crew. The holidays might be coming, but I know for sure we won't have time to enjoy them.

"We haven't started and I'm already tired," whispers Greg, who is sitting next to me.

"Maybe you should party less and sleep more," I whisper back.

And maybe I should listen to my own advice. I'm also exhausted, although deliciously so. Having Commander Thunder waiting for me in bed, with all his guns ready to fire, is beginning to put a dent on my energy levels. I need a good night's sleep, without wandering hands waking me at dawn, searching for all my secret places.

Shit, just thinking about him gets me excited. This is going from bad to worse, Adrik is driving me crazy, and my head is bursting thinking about what he'll do next to surprise me. We have done so many things, and I'm not just talking about in bed, not everything is about sex, no matter how good that side of things is.

We had a candlelight dinner in his living room, slowly feeding each other with our fingers, savoring the taste of the food on our skin. Never has something as simple as whipped cream tasted so good to me.

We also went dancing, went to the movies and even out riding his bike around the city a couple of times, coming back home hot and bothered. Adrik also tried to get me out surfing with him a few times, but that was a lost cause. This time of year the water is way too cold for my taste, even wearing a wet suit.

I dream of going back to Hawaii with him, we can build a lot of happy memories in my beloved islands.

"Hey there, Zanetti," Anderson calls to get my attention, snapping his fingers.

"I was making a list of everything I still need to read up about before going to the base library. Do you have any extra info you could share?"

As if reading my thoughts, the captain speaks.

"We've decided to surprise you. We want you to make your plans thinking about what we've been working on this week, while also preparing for the unexpected and unpredictable scenarios."

"Sir," calls out Vargas. "How are we supposed to make detailed plans when we haven't been told our assigned vessel yet?"

"You'll have to use your initiative, along with a lot of planning. You must abide by the allocated budget while also managing with the available resources. You have plenty of time to complete your homework before setting sail, but there is a lot of work to do, so try not to waste your time."

"Tell that to Zanetti, she's been wasting her time all over the base," I hear whispered.

I'm going to kill Vargas, my classmate is such an idiot. I give him the stink eye and the man shuts his mouth.

"What Zanetti does or doesn't do in her spare time is not your problem, Lieutenant Vargas. I suggest you put your neurons to work on something more productive in order to deliver the projects you've been given by Monday, since you're the only one running late."

The biting reply of our instructor is followed by a round of jeers and Vargas, who had no right to poke his nose into my private life, is left with no choice but to walk away with his tail between his legs.

"Are you ready?" Adrik smiles as he taps the code into the small code pad.

God, he looks good in the black shirt he's wearing with dark jeans. After Thanksgiving, Adrik announced he was moving into his townhouse, so here we are. My man wants to show me his place, and we've agreed this weekend will be all about planning, then next weekend we'll go furniture hunting. We're standing at his door, his truck is parked by the curb. This is downtown, but the street is quiet and very nice. From the outside, his house looks modern, all concrete and clean lines. I'm loving it already.

"You're the one inviting me into his dream home." I smile back. "Maybe you should be nervous, maybe I'll like the house so much I'll decide to invade it and then what'll you do with me?"

His smile lets me know that wouldn't be a problem.

This man...

"Oh, I can think of a couple of things, but the question is whether my brave girl is ready for the challenge," he answers before kissing my lips and opening the door.

And I'm more than ready to accept whatever comes.

Adrik, like the gentleman that he is, lets me go first as we enter a small hall, and what I see there steals my breath.

"Whoa..." I murmur.

The house isn't that big, but it's well laid out. Wooden floors and a large open space with high ceilings give it an industrial feel, and I love everything about this place.

My head is already spinning with possibilities.

Having breakfast in the kitchen—with Adrik cooking, of course—while I spend my time ogling him and sipping coffee.

Eating dinner on a rug in the living room, eating with chopsticks directly from the boxes.

Running up the stairs on the left, breathing hard while we can't stop kissing, stumbling on the steps.

Why am I having all these thoughts about being—and living—here with him? He asked my help, not to overstep.

"You like what you see?" He sounds hesitant, shy almost.

"I love it," I answer truthfully. "Now that I'm here, I'm wondering what the hell you're doing living at the base? Your place is cool and all, but I would have moved in here as soon as I disembarked."

"I was waiting for a certain dark-eyed brunette to come and keep me company," he says, hugging me from behind, pressing me up against his hard chest. "Plus, as you can see, this place is empty; I don't even have a blow up mattress here."

I throw my head back and lean against his shoulder, giving him access to nuzzle my neck.

"So you were hunting me down purely to use me as your interior decorator?"

"I asked you for some pics to hang on the walls so you could be my home *decoration.*"

"Don't be so crude, Adrik."

"I'm being honest, there's a difference. I want you as a permanent home fixture."

"Don't you think you're going too fast, Commander?"

He laughs as he nibbles my ear with his lips.

"Jordania, are you really going back to your apartment? Can you honestly say you won't miss me as much I'll miss being around you every day?"

Well, I guess he has a point. And with regard to my apartment, I've never put much in it, just my clothes and my beautiful coffee maker.

"Adrik, you can't seriously be asking me to come and live here with you," I say, already very tempted to answer yes. However, this is an important decision which shouldn't be rushed in the heat of a sex induced fever.

"Why the hell not?"

"Because you bought this house thinking about the future, to make it your home. What'll happen if it doesn't work out between us?"

But thinking about another woman being here with him crushes me, I don't want him to be with anyone but me. I'm confused and a storm of doubts turns my mind upside down.

And then his words blow away all the doubts and make me soar.

"I think that instead of worrying about all the bad things that could happen, we should concentrate on the good." He takes a deep breath. "Jordania, I'm in love with you and I want to make long-term plans with you. Give us a chance, take a risk on being happy with me."

He's killing me.

"Adrik…" I murmur softly, as one of his hands sneaks under the waistband of my pants.

"Say yes, my beautiful warrior. That day at the pier, I asked you to be brave and let me love you. Jump with me, let go of the rope and say yes."

Swoon.

"Don't you think I should tell you something first?" I ask, moving my hips, looking for his naughty fingers and also for the erection that is pressing against my butt.

"Depends if I'm going to like it."

"So you don't want to hear that I'm in love with you?"

He freezes behind me, I'm not sure that he's even breathing.

"Really?" he asks incredulously, turning me in his arms to look me in the eye. "Is what you just said true?"

"I wouldn't lie about something so important, Adrik," I state, gently kissing his lips.

He lets out the big breath that he's been holding in.

"I'm so fucking happy right now, and so in love with you." He tenderly kisses me back. "So, are you coming to live here with me?"

He rests his forehead on mine, and we are so close and not just physically. I think my whole heart has taken root in the warmth of his love.

The best place to be.

Forever.

"One step at a time. Why don't we see how much effort you're prepared to make to convince me?" I murmur.

Without giving me the chance to say any more, he takes my hand and leads me up the stairs to the second floor, to an empty room.

"Too bad there's no bed in here," I tell him, not sure what's on his mind.

"Who needs one?" He pulls me into the room, leaving a trail of clothes behind us, ending up behind the tempered glass screen of the attached bathroom.

We hug in silence under the jets of warm water, my skin vibrating to the rhythm of his touch, his kisses. It's not just about giving him my body, we are sharing everything now.

Shortly after, when I have my back against the cold gray granite of the wall, as my hands urgently seek him out, his eyes tell me everything I need to know. There are moments in life that are important, solemn, transcendental. This is one of those moments and neither of us wants to spoil it with words.

The space soon fills with steam and our gasps, mine asking for more, his begging for me. A quick onslaught becomes two, then I lose count along with all sense of reality, lost in the moment and everything he's offering me. His strength, his courage, his love.

All of him.

Adrik.

My fingers travel down his shoulders, through the thick lines of ink that cover one of them, devouring him, telling him how much I want him, how much I love him.

His hands clench my hips and the craving grows as I reach my limit. This is too much, he is too much, pleasure, love and need mingle, driving me up to fly, and also bonding me to him.

There are no rules to be broken here.

Just he and I becoming one.

Forever.

"We need to get out of this shower," he finally says.

I'm perfectly content here, although my fingers are a bit pruney now.

Adrik looks at his wristwatch and then moves quickly to turn off the shower. Trust me, this is a total turn off, the water still feels divine.

"Hey! We're still fine here, where's the fire?"

"We have somewhere else to be," he explains.

"You're full of surprises today, Commander." My words sound like a purr, I'm saying yes to another place as long as it involves us naked and alone.

I can't get enough of my man.

"You have no idea," he says as he gets out of the shower, returning shortly with a towel.

"Seems like you had some stuff concealed in this house, Houston, how did you do it?"

"A good magician never reveals his secrets."

"Too many secrets for my taste today. So, where are you taking me?"

"I'm not saying anything." He leans on the bathroom counter gloriously naked while I'm drying myself with the only towel we have at hand.

A cloud of steam surrounds us, the mist of our love and the passion we share swaddling us.

"I hope you aren't taking me to a ball or something. I have very little makeup in my purse and you've made me messy as hell."

"I like you messy, and I very much like being messy with you," he smirks.

"You are not being a gentleman," I whine. Why won't he tell me where we're going?

He stares but still tells me nothing, not a single word comes from his lips.

"Remember what I said that day at the waterfall?"

"Huh?"

"I told you I'm always the villain in the story, never Prince Charming."

"Lucky for both of us that I've never wanted a man to come and rescue me wearing white tights."

"What about a white uniform?"

"Now you're talking my language. Houston, come and talk dirty to me."

The towel is hanging from my hand, so he takes it from me and quickly dries his short hair, an easy task to accomplish.

I'll never get enough of the way his muscles move beneath his olive skin. This is my very own porn movie.

And my romance flick.

Adrik heads to the bedroom, but turns to look at me over his shoulder.

"Let's be clear, you don't need Prince Charming coming to the rescue. I have no doubt that you're smart enough, and strong enough to look after yourself, so you'd better believe it, Jordania."

Talk about powerful words... this man and his silver tongue, he could sell ice cream to the Eskimos.

My hair is mostly dry, so I turn my ponytail into a messy bun, leaving a few strands around my face. A few minutes later, I'm spritzing my wrist with perfume while walking down the stairs, as a knock sounds across the empty house.

"Brother," Adrik says to someone. "Yes, we're on our way."

Another man is there with him in the foyer. A tall, lean, smart blonde guy with striking eyes and smile from ear to ear.

"Here she is," Adrik announces while taking my hand.

Both men smile at me, one with eyes full of pride, the other with a face full of wonder.

Who is this man?

"Babe, this is Lancelot Hills, my brother from another mother," Adrik explains. "Lance, this is Jordania Zanetti, my girlfriend."

"It's a pleasure finally meeting you, Jordania. You're the answer to my aunt's prayers, and we've been looking forward to meeting you."

"Behave," Adrik warns his friend, but his tone is playful and his smile hasn't faded.

"And talking about being well-behaved, my little mermaid is on full dragon mode. She sent me to look for you, and I advise you not to cross her," he adds with a laugh. "We're planning a big Christmas party, you are coming, right? Morgana is moving to the city and Percival and my aunt are coming too."

Lancelot, Morgana, Percival, in what century are we living? Those names are pretty old-fashioned and unique.

"Well, it seems that after the New Year, you will have new neighbors," Adrik replies proudly.

"Neighbors?" Lancelot queries, raising his eyebrows. "As in plural?"

"As in plural."

"Jordania, blink twice if you're being forced to move in or something. We can help you."

"Don't be stupid, Lancelot." Adrik rolls his eyes. "I've made sure she's happy to move in, right, babe?"

Lancelot just laughs while we all walk to his home.

"Tell me a bit more about you, Jordania. Where are you from?"

"Born in Virginia, raised in many places," I answer.

Lancelot frowns, not understanding my reply.

"Military daughter," Adrik explains, shrugging.

"This deserves a celebration. The whole gang is here, waiting for you to have dinner. Ariel made your favorite, chocolate crepe cake, just for you, you lucky motherfucker."

Adrik smiles at me, his hand holding mine, with so much love in his eyes it leaves me breathless.

Rule # 15: Find a strong woman whose heart isn't afraid to love, and whose wings aren't afraid to fly.

Chapter
FIFTEEN

Laughter can be heard as soon as the door opens. There's a large wreath with the colors of autumn hanging, plus some pots on either side filled with multicolored flowers, giving the impression of a happy, cheerful home.

Lancelot signals for us to wait a minute before entering, which we happily do, eager to surprise.

"Finally!" a male voice calls out good-humoredly. "Your wife threatened to starve us until you came back with your friend."

"That is not true!" From where we stand, I can't see much of his wife, just a glimpse of her white blonde hair. "God, Holland, I don't know how poor Rosie puts up with you."

"Aw, my poor, wife," the man replies. "Don't you worry, I always make sure she's taken care of."

I feel a pang of envy. I've never been part of a close group of friends that tease each other in such a relaxed and easy manner. Other than Casper, I only have my colleagues.

When I hear a baby happily babbling, I know I'm right, this is a happy home, you can just feel all the happy vibes.

"I have a surprise for you, Hummingbird," Lancelot calls out. "Look who I just found."

"Ta-da!" Adrik exclaims playfully, while I just go with the flow as Lancelot beckons us into the room.

The blonde girl stares open-mouthed at us from her husband's arms, holding a giggling baby boy between them. Their child inherited his mother's amazing gray eyes, but otherwise he is a carbon copy of his father. He's gorgeous, although with those genes, it's hardly surprising.

"Well, it's as if Lazarus has risen," she exclaims, throwing herself into Adrik's arms, who by some miracle manages to catch her without letting go of my hand, before she smashes her head against the wall.

Thankfully the baby is safe in his father's arms.

"Better than Lazarus," says Adrik. "I was never dead."

"The next time you disappear for so long, I might send someone to do the job," she replies laughing. "Your nephew has grown so much and you missed it."

"That is one thing I do regret," he apologizes. "But the good news is that at the end of the year, we'll be moving into a house nearby, so you'll be able to scold me whenever you want."

"Oh my God," she cries. "What an impression we must be giving, I'm sorry, we don't normally tend to be so rude. I'm Ariel Hills."

"And this, little mermaid, is my girlfriend, Jordania Zanetti, and your new neighbor." Adrik smiles.

Ariel's shrieks so loudly it's only by God's grace that she doesn't leave us deaf, before hugging me and planting a kiss on my cheek.

"Come on, I have to introduce you. We have a lot to talk about, we're planning a big Christmas party this year... of course you're both invited..." Ariel says breathlessly, pulling me over to the couch where another couple is sitting looking at each other, with big smiles painted on their faces.

"We have new neighbors," Ariel informs them as if they just didn't hear. "Isn't that exciting? Finally Adrik is moving into the neighborhood. We have to celebrate. Lancelot, get the wine out of the fridge."

"I'm on it," he replies, walking toward the kitchen. "Adrik, do you want a beer?"

"Hey, I know you." The woman on the couch smiles as I approach.

Small world—turns out she's the owner of the bakery I went to some weeks ago.

I'm still stunned when she winks and says, "From the looks of things, I'm guessing you got your mess sorted."

Ariel comes and stands by my side, looking between Roselynn and I.

"You've met before?" she asks indignantly. "Why did I not know about this?"

"I went into the bakery a few weeks ago, and we started talking," I explain.

"Yeah, we talked a lot," Roselynn nods. "If only I'd known the guy you were talking about was Adrik…"

"Well, we know now, and I want the full story. Spill the tea, girl!" Ariel orders as she sits in a big overstuffed chair with her legs tucked under her lithe body.

"So, I'm here to give you both the scoop?" I laugh.

"Don't mind her," says Roselynn, resting a hand on her growing belly. She looks so cute, pregnancy really suits her. She's glowing. "Come on, talk to me."

"Behave and mind your manners, or there'll be no cake for you, pregnant lady," Ariel chides. "And this morning I made this new recipe with clementine oranges and dark chocolate."

Roselynn groans, I'm not sure if it is from craving the cake or having to share the intel.

"Jordania, this is Ariel, my best friend and business partner. You can talk with her as freely as you did with me."

"That's my good girl." Ariel winks, a triumphant smile on her lips.

Chatting with them is easy, and fun too, they're obviously thick as thieves yet they don't make me feel like an outsider.

Roselynn and Ariel tell me about their bakery and ask a lot about my work, general things, mostly.

"Jordania," Lancelot says after a while as we're sitting around the table in their eclectic dining room, enjoying the most delicious crepe cake with berries, a wonderful combination of sweet and tart. "If you ever get tired of hanging around with this stupid ass, I have a brother I can introduce you to."

"Fuck you, Hills," Adrik immediately retorts. "Find another woman for Percival, this beauty is off the market."

"Is that so? I don't see any ring on my finger," I answer playfully. "I'm a free woman, free as the wind."

"Don't give me ideas, Vegas is just a four hour drive," he murmurs in my ear, so only I hear. "Feeling adventurous?"

No freaking way, one step at a time.

"Behave!" I give him a hard nudge.

"A man can dream…"

This girl might be starting to dream too, but this isn't the right time.

"So, you've finally found your match," Chase tells Adrik. "It's nice to see you happy, it was about time. But it did take us by surprise."

"No more than me," my commander replies, his gaze locking with mine as he does so.

"Another beer?" Lancelot asks.

"No thanks, I've had my lot for tonight since I'll be driving back to the base," he says, even though I'm sure he'd love to accept.

But he's proving to be a responsible man, one able to exert self-control.

"Easy, Houston, we don't have a problem here," I say. "I've only had lemonade, so go ahead if you want another beer, I can drive us back."

His face lights up instantly.

God, he's about to let me handle his baby, Adrik adores his truck.

If we didn't have such a large audience, I'd show my appreciation of the tremendous vote of confidence he's just given me.

"Hills, where's that beer?" Adrik orders, before kissing me in front of everyone.

After spending some time with Arthur, the son of Ariel and Lancelot, my allergy to young children subsides, and I don't know if it's because I'm feeling so happy right now, or if it's the maternal urge I thought I was missing is finally kicking in. I say goodbye to little Arthur before his mother puts him to bed, with a new yearning that maybe someday I can have something so precious in my arms.

Adrik has mentioned wanting children, but we never really talked about it. Is it still something he's planning on? And, more importantly, will he want to have them with me?

As we leave, I say something that's been on my mind.

"You know, since we left your house I have been thinking…"

"It's *our* house, Jordania, get used to it."

Despite his tone, his serious statement makes me smile.

"Well, since we left *our* house," I begin again with my speech. "I've been thinking. Can we sleep in my apartment tonight?"

He turns to stare at me, surprised by my request.

"Why are you so nervous about us moving in together?"

"Actually, I was thinking it would be more like a farewell," I explain. "If I give notice to leave my apartment, we could maybe celebrate the new year in our new home."

A wide smile is drawn on Adrik's handsome face, he's thrilled with what I just suggested.

"Do we have to wait until the end of the month?"

"You can always try to convince me otherwise."

"You just said the magic words, Lieutenant," he whispers, stroking my thigh, and even through the corduroy of my brick-colored pants, his heat burns me. "Put your foot down on that accelerator, we're in a hurry!"

"Wake up, beautiful," Adrik whispers as he leaves a trail of kisses along my neck. "We have a lot to do."

"It's Sunday, Adrik. We don't need to get up early today," I groan in protest. "Go back to sleep."

Last night we arrived back at almost one o'clock in the morning, stumbling into my apartment, shedding our clothes along the way, until we fell naked in the cold bed sheets.

The sheets are wrinkled now and smell of sex and us. My body hurts, yes, hurts, but in the right way and in the right places. I don't think even the arduous training that the SEALs are subjected to could have prepared me for what happened between us last night. Nor could anything have prepared me for what it's like giving myself, body and soul, to someone that I am sure loves me with all his heart.

I'm sick, love sick, and I don't want to be healed.

"Hold on tight," Adrik told me just before he slid his erection through my wet folds.

Where did he intend me to hold on? The only place I could find were his ink covered shoulders before I got carried away by ecstasy.

After that I think I fell asleep or maybe I fainted, I'm not sure. I just know that my skin craved Adrik's hot body, while he occupied himself making love to me slowly.

"Come on, my love," he repeats, stretching over my body like a cat, forcing my legs apart with his.

"And this is how you intend to make me get up?" I gasp.

The world stops spinning, time stops, I forget fatigue, and everything else as his rapid movements unleash an impetuous storm inside me. I cling to him tightly, shouting his name, begging for more.

"Why the hell did I think this was a good idea?" I ask hours later, as I close my second suitcase.

Of course, Commander Houston, impatient as always, doesn't want to wait another minute to have me at home, at his beck and call. Despite my groans, he got up, and began packing my clothes in the first suitcase he found in the closet, so I had to get up and finish the task.

"It was you who wanted to go home," he replies. "I'm only obeying your wishes to keep you happy."

"Is this how you're going to be about everything?"

"With all your wishes?" He raises his eyebrows. "Yes, sir. My top priority is always to see you happy."

Can one resist a statement like that? Of course not.

I love him and I'm not ashamed to admit it.

"I don't know how sharing a house with you will turn out," I confess, hugging him as I rest my head on his shoulder. "Yesterday Ariel was handling everything so efficiently, but I don't know if I'm going to be able to do that."

I have no idea about cooking or decorating. Sure, I'm tidy but that's not enough.

"Jordania," he says firmly, taking me by the shoulders to look him in the eye. My hands grip his arms, I need to touch him, I have to, to be able to breathe.

He is my air, the oxygen that fuels this fire that runs through my veins.

"I chose you, you are the one I want. It was my heart who decided to love you, but my free will that has taken the reins. This is not the impulse of a crazy teenager, and I don't want you to be the perfect housewife, I just want you to be you. Stubborn, bossy, and so freaking beautiful that I get blinded by you."

"Wow," I sigh. "That's a long list of faults."

Hopefully he also has a list of my virtues, because surely there must be a few.

"I love you because of who you are, faults and all, Jordania," he replies, his eyes fixed on mine, radiating sincerity. "I don't intend to change you, I fell in love with you for who you are, and every time you're not close to me I feel like a man wandering alone, lost in the desert. I keep finding myself staring at the wall, just thinking of you. You're my solace, Jordania, but

262 ⚡

my eyes are wide open and I'm not in love with any kind of a mirage."

"Tell me who you are and what you have done with my Commander Houston."

He laughs, a deep sound that reverberates in his chest.

"I'm the same person I always was," he declares. "Only now I'm in love."

In love with me.

Rule #16: Looking for the perfect gift? What about giving yourself to her completely, unabashedly, and to the end of time.

Chapter
SIXTEEN

So here we are.

Standing hand in hand in the huge parking lot of the infamous Swedish furniture store, ready to overcome this latest challenge.

Yesterday as I googled all the different options for the things we need, my nerves spiked as I realized this wasn't going to be a child's game, more like a battlefield hidden inside the royal blue walls of this massive building.

"You ready?" Adrik has a cart in front of him, ready to go.

"As ready as I'll ever be." The truth is I'm not sure that I am, but what the heck, we are moving in together next week. We both have five free days and are planning to take advantage of them to the max. We have a long list of basic requirements we need to get, thanks to Adrik's idea about hosting a Christmas brunch for his grandparents.

Hold the cavalry, nope, I'm not cooking, we hired a catering company to supply the food at our new nest, so all we need now is a festive centerpiece. Thank God for the wonders of this era.

I invited my father too, or at least I tried to, but the high and mighty Admiral Zanetti is always busy—no surprises there—so I was forced to leave a message with his secretary, to which he has yet to respond. Previously, I'd have been seriously upset by this, but right now I have far too much to do. There are walls to paint, clothes to pack, and love to make.

Even my beloved Hawaiian fireworks are forgotten. I'm sure my Commander Houston will make me see shooting stars without leaving the bed.

If someone had dared to tell me a couple of months ago that at the end of the year I'd be planning to move in with my new boyfriend, I would have laughed so loud, and yet now, here I am in the flesh and blood, about to do just that.

There are so many horror stories about this store we're about to enter. Some say it's a sure recipe for a relationship meltdown, and not to be tackled by novices, but despite it all, here we are.

Bring it on!

I'm clutching a long list of necessities in my hand—a notepad containing the measurements of our house, two pens, and a highlighter, and a cell phone full of pictures. Last week, we bought our living *and* dining room furniture, but the list is still so long, and it seems we have barely scratched the surface.

"Shall we?" Adrik makes a move forward, while I remain glued to the spot, looking up at the large yellow store name.

"Do you think we'll survive this?"

The way he smiles at me makes my body melt and my brain go mushy. It's like Adrik has mastered this thing about navigating the relationship ocean with ease, while I'm still trying to learn how to paddle in a rowboat.

"Babe, we'll rock this. Forged by the sea, right?"

Oh boy, if only I had his optimism, folks say war is an easier business. "Or will we end up calling a therapist?"

"Nah, this will be fun." He grins confidently.

We enter the store and after fifteen minutes I'm overwhelmed.

Too many sizes, colors, and options.

And so many people walking around. Plus, I swear I just saw a man sleeping in a nursery display.

We wander through the crowded aisles, the only beacon of light on this journey is watching Adrik's fine ass in those jeans he's wearing. Every time he gives me one of his smiles, my heart beats faster, and I can't help but wonder if this feeling will ever get old. I really hope it won't, being in love isn't as terrible as single people make it out to be. He erases my bad memories, everything else pales in comparison to this, all the old pictures fade because he's filling my world with bright colors, with love and utter happiness.

Next time I'll have to bring a couple of tissues boxes, so many girls are drooling over my man. I'm tempted to use the fly swatter in my cart to shoo them away.

We're standing in front of a really cool bedroom display. The light wood would go perfectly with the dark blue paint on our walls, the design is modern and clean, with a retro appeal.

"I think they have this one in king size," I say, while Adrik frowns as he looks at the bed.

"You mean for the guest room?"

"No, I was thinking for our room, Adrik. Now that we looked at all the options here, I think this one is the best."

"We aren't buying our bed here. You can forget that nonsense."

I look at the contents of our cart, figuring out what's heavier. I need to get it through his thick skull that I'm fed up, tired, and we still don't have a bed.

"You said you didn't want to spend our first night at the new house sleeping on a blow up mattress on the floor."

The way he looks at me makes me feel like a child about to be scolded.

"We're going to need something much sturdier than that. Just look at those stupid little screws and flimsy thin wooden planks. I don't want to end up on the floor mid fuck."

Those words, that voice, those smoky eyes set me on fire. I no longer care about the stupid bed, I just want to go back home and ride him like a champ to the moon and back.

Hard.

"Well, Commander, we have two options. Buy the bed here or go to Target and get ready to blow."

At my words a slow smile appears on his handsome face.

"I'm always ready for you to blow me, babe. If it requires a trip to Target, so be it. I promise you'll be well rewarded afterwards."

As I look at our full cart and weigh up our options, Adrik smirks at me.

"I have a third winning option. Let's go back home, then when you're thoroughly fucked and in a better mood, we'll look online for a bed. I'm tired of crowded stores. People get crazy around the holidays."

Online shopping, magic words.

"Take me home, Houston."

"It will be my pleasure."

After fifty minutes of waiting in line, we finally get out of the store. Every time another item pinged on the register I flinched, but Adrik didn't even blink. While he pushes the cart on our way to his truck, I'm so focused on the receipt that I don't notice a couple of skaters coming my way at full speed until it's too late.

"Jordania," Adrik yells to get my attention. "Watch out!"

He pushes me out of the way with so much force that I end up in one of the flowerbeds, stuck between the plants and bushes. This is not my best look, the local flora doesn't suit me.

My cheek hurts so freaking much, as well as my head. I try to stand up and end up back on the floor.

Why am I so dizzy? Is it lack of food or excitement about surviving the Swedish challenge?

"Babe, don't move," Adrik says while checking me over from head to toe. "I should take you to the hospital to get checked out."

Seeing him so concerned makes me smile even when my head is about to explode, I've become the incarnation of the mind-blowing emoji. Suddenly my brain is turning into an expanding mass compressed by my skull.

"I just wanna go home," I murmur, my voice barely audible.

"Can you stand?" he asks, still looking worried.

"Yes, but you need to take care of all the stuff we bought today, otherwise we'll have to come back to this wretched place and start all over again."

Adrik's gaze is fixated on me, like my words are some kind of crazy talk.

"I don't care about any of that stuff," he states.

"Don't you dare leave them. Just grab our things. I'll walk to the truck. I'm perfectly fine."

"At least you still have your wits."

Ignoring his sarcasm, I manage to stand and walk, it's not that hard, I mastered the ability before turning one, after all.

Oh what better way to spread the cheer on Christmas Eve Eve than in the hospital waiting for a doctor to check my foot, surrounded by the smell of alcohol and floor disinfectant, while Adrik terrorizes the nursing staff about paging the doctor faster, getting my X-Rays results quicker etc… etc…

The bruise on my cheek doesn't feel that bad, but it looks worse and worse by the minute. Half my face is turning purple, even with the help of the frozen gel pack a terrified nurse brought me an hour ago. She must deal with stubborn sailors every day, but I can't imagine any of them being half as intimidating as *my* commander.

His contrite face almost makes me laugh.

"I am sorry," he says for the thirtieth time. "I was so careless, I did not think things through. I am the worst boyfriend in the world, all those years of training went straight to the garbage…"

"Hey," I stop him before he can continue. All the way to the hospital he has been apologizing, and I have to admit that I felt my heart full of love just hearing him, even when I know it wasn't *his fault*.

"It was my fault. I was so worried about the crazy amount of money you spent that I was not paying attention while walking. And you like the great Commander that you are, assessed the situation, and did what you thought was best. And you reacted fast, get over it, Thunder."

He gives me a weak smile and I know that my words had no effect as he still blames himself.

"Look at us," I say to try to lighten the mood, as he closely inspects my swollen ankle for the millionth time. "The very definition of a power couple, eh? You're marching around like a bull in a China shop while I'm such a weakling I can't even stand on my own two feet."

I'm trying to lighten the atmosphere a little but Commander Houston isn't amused at all.

"Don't put yourself down, you have amazing inner strength, Jordania," he insists. "Doesn't matter that you can't walk right now, because you're more than a couple of bruises and a sprained ankle. You shine every fucking single day of your life, because it's in your marrow, deep in your bones. And I'm the lucky motherfucker that gets to hold your hand, stand beside you, and *that* is what makes us a power couple. Don't you dare to forget it."

My body aches for a different reason, my entire being longs for him. Only this incredible man can make me forget this shitty situation. I'm not just breathing, I'm alive, and that's because of him.

Finally I'm allowed to leave sporting the latest shoe trend—AKA an ankle splint—we arrived home past midnight, dead tired, and hungry.

"Zeph came by earlier to assemble my old bed for us, so everything's ready."

We had planned to spend the night at our new home bragging about our success at the Swedish furniture store, drinking wine, and painting the coal grey wall in our dining room, but those plans changed thanks to my accident.

"He left some take-out in the oven, so I'm going to fix a plate for you. Then like a good girl, you're going to take all your pills and sleep tight until tomorrow morning." Oh, a gal could get used to this five-star service.

But as exhausted I am, I'm never too tired to be stubborn, and I still want to argue about his fussing, but my sassy reply dies on the tip of my tongue when I realize how tired he is, and yet here he is, always putting me first. Could any words speak louder? I really don't think so.

After being fed and carried in my man's arms to our bedroom, I sleep like a baby. Waking up in a cozy, warm cocoon, I could do this every single day without ever getting bored. Adrik's strong chest provides the best pillow ever.

"It's past noon," he says in that deep voice I love so much. "Are you hungry?"

Still in a sleepy fog, my brain tries to work out how I'm feeling. No, I'm not hungry, my ankle aches, so does my head but we have a lot to do today. After all, it's Christmas Eve and we haven't wrapped a single gift. We're going to a big party at the Hill's home tonight and then we are hosting for Adrik's grandparents tomorrow.

My heart hurts more than my body—I miss the family I've never had. My father didn't pick up my calls, so this year it'll be just me.

We need to run to the huge craft store to pick up the table centerpiece for tomorrow and then wrap as if we're North Pole trained elves. There's no time to waste.

"Where are you going?" Adrik asks when I attempt to get up, but failed as I have a steel band around my waist. Please read one of my man's arms, and it doesn't bulge.

"We have plans, Houston. Let me move." And those crutches lying on the floor will be my best friends for the next two weeks. Doctor's words, not mine.

"Yes, babe, we do indeed have plans, none of which include you running errands around the city. Just stay put and let me take care of you," Adrik adamantly insists.

Okay. I guess the agenda just got cleared.

We spend our evening having dinner on the living room rug, eating Thai food, laughing, and telling silly stories while making plans for our future.

"Come to Hawaii with me," I suggest, when we talk about our next vacation.

"Don't you wanna go to another exotic place? Somewhere new for the both of us, Thailand, Croatia?

"No, no, I want to explore the island with you. Staying in my home and just wandering around. Once I finish this training course, I think we'll both need some downtime."

He smiles, but there is something else. The man is hatching something, I can tell.

"Talking about Hawaii…" He gets up and heads to the kitchen, then returns with a wooden crate. "This should do the trick."

From the crate, Adrik produces a little blowtorch, sugar, some metal sticks, and cinnamon, then finally a pineapple.

"There you go," he proudly announces.

"You know…" Oh yes, two can play at this game. "Just because you have a pineapple doesn't make this Hawaiian."

He laughs at my serious face. Well, I'm joking… *kinda…*

"But you know how fond I am of pineapples, right?"

That joke never gets old…

And talking about fruits with thick skin, a crown, and sweet on the inside... I do love it with a mix of sugar and cinnamon, then blasting it with a blowtorch.

The pineapple is such an underestimated fruit in the romantic field.

"Fuck," Adrik groans as he picks up his phone when it rings.

Yesterday was just for us, no cell phones or laptops around. Just the two of us enjoying our first Christmas together. Me being carried around the house while Adrik fussed over me, putting everything together for the family gathering.

And talking about family, who's on the phone? It's pretty early to call.

"They are where?" He smiles. "Lancelot's crazy, and he can't blame Ariel for this. Yes, please, call him to let him know. Thanks, Herrera, *Feliz navidad.*"

Adrik ends the call and comes to sit beside me on the couch, I'm tying bows for the brand new tree Adrik found tucked away in a forgotten corner of Target.

The thing didn't come with a base, can you believe it? So he had to improvise, but life isn't about being perfect. It's about making the best with the cards you've been dealt.

"What happened with Lancelot and Ariel?" I turn to ask him.

"Ariel was having a rough time, so he surprised her by moving the whole crew to Big Bear." He scratches his stubble, as if thinking about how to up his game.

Adrik has nothing to worry about, my Christmas has been great, sprained ankle and all.

"Zephyr is driving up there right now. I invited him here, but he said having snow would make a nice change."

"Thank God we aren't going. Big Bear at this time of year is too cold for these used-to-live-in-Hawaii bones."

He pulls me over to sit on his lap. Yes, this is a great place to be, and I don't even need to move my foot.

"Don't move that way, babe, you're giving him hope," he indicates his growing boner beneath my butt, and I kinda like that this part of his anatomy has his own brain. "And sadly we don't have time, the catering service will be here soon and then we'll be hosting my grandparents. We'd better go hop in the shower."

We end up in the bathtub instead of the shower—a good decision, I must add. However, we take so long that when the catering service arrives, Adrik has to run and open the door wearing just his gray sweatpants. By the time I make it to the kitchen, I'm tempted to provide our chef with some napkins so the poor girl can mop up the drool wetting her chin.

I can't blame her, and she can ogle as much as she wants, but there'll be no touching or flirting. The man is off the market for good, *so back off, bitch.*

Adrik's grandparents are so sweet. After the great thanksgiving we had, I was ecstatic to spend Christmas with them, and the cherry on top is that Luana is having a good day. She recognizes her grandson and takes great pride as he shows her around the house.

"I know what you did for us, my sweet boy," she says while we're eating. "You went and enlisted straight after school, and you didn't do it just to keep yourself occupied. You did it because you wanted to help us with the money."

Luana stands and hugs Adrik, and there is so much love around the table. This family takes care of their own, they love each other deeply, and that's the reason Adrik fought for me, to take care of me and why he keeps doing so every single day.

And that breaks the dam, I can't take it. Seriously, I can't.

I don't know how I'm breathing in this fucking moment.

I need to leave, the air around the house is suffocating me.

Limping, I walk to the foyer and open the door. When the cold breeze hits me I feel grateful for it. I'm hyperventilating, having a massive panic attack. The reason? I feel like a tree with no roots. The prestige, the last name, the reputation means nothing. Nothing. And that's the only thing I have in my kit. What can I possibly bring to this relationship since I came into this world with nothing to give?

Balancing my body against the rail on our little porch, I remain there until a strong arm slips rounds my waist.

"What are you doing out here, baby?" His voice is low, gentle, as if he knows what's going on inside my head.

"What are we doing, Adrik?"

"I don't know about you, but I'm eating my weight in berry strudel." He moves to carry me back into the warm interior.

"No, Adrik, you don't understand." I struggle to free myself from his grip, but he doesn't make it easy.

Damn man and his strength.

"Then make me understand."

"Can't you see? You're surrounded with so much love, I feel like I've just been grafted on. This isn't my place, being with you. You deserve better, Adrik, you deserve to be with a woman with a loving family to mingle with yours."

He stares at me as if suddenly I lost my freaking mind.

"Fuck that, it's not what I want. I want you. You think you don't deserve *me?* Baby, I wake up every single day feeling like the luckiest motherfucker in the world because the prettiest, smartest, and funniest woman dared to look at me and give me a chance."

Hell, why am I such a crying, shaking mess? I barely recognize myself.

"Stop it, Jordania. Enough. I know you're missing your father, but if you're lost at sea, then let me be your north star, let me bring you home, baby. Lean on me."

This man...

I collapse against his chest, discovering all over again that Adrik gives the best hugs in the entire world.

"Let's go back inside. My Nana is going to torture you with more stories about me being a teenager, so brace yourself."

I let him carry me back in, and then we literally eat our weight in sweets and drink coffee while opening our gifts.

I got Adrik a book about the Battle of Midway. The man loves naval history, and this is a present he can open in public. Yes, I'm being naughty and inside a cute envelope in the bedroom I have those pictures he's been asking me for since we met.

Adrik gives me a single pearl on a thin gold chain. "To match your mother's earrings."

And although it's beautiful and thoughtful, I don't need jewelry.

I just need him. That's all I'll ever need.

Adrik Houston is the best gift life gave me, ever.

Rule # 17: Be a man of few words. There are lots of better ways to use your tongue.

Chapter
SEVENTEEN

"Don't be nervous," he tells me as I'm sitting on the bathroom counter. "Everything will be fine."

He's shaving and as the razor skims his sun-kissed skin, I wonder why this is so freaking sexy. Being here with him is one of our new routines.

Every day we share our morning shower, then while I finish up, he shaves and grooms in front of the big mirror. We've been living together for almost two months now and I still can't quite believe it.

I swear I don't look half as sexy as he does while I'm shaving my armpits.

This is my very own porn movie. And to think we'll be separated by miles of ocean over the weekend.

I'll miss him, that's for sure.

"How do you know it'll be fine?" Oh my God, today we begin the exercises at sea, and I don't have a clue about which vessel I've been assigned to, not a fucking clue. "A thousand things could come up, Adrik. Like, what if the commander of the destroyer doesn't like me?"

He laughs and walks over and takes me in his strong arms. This is my favorite place to be in the whole wide world.

Yes, I've lost my fucking mind. I'm so in love with this wonderful man.

"Have confidence in what you've been working on and you'll do just fine," he murmurs, stroking my back. "The commander assigned to you will be delighted—who could resist all this?"

Emphasizing his words, his hands travel to the curve of my butt. My body instantly craves his, but we don't have time now. Living away from the base has a lot of advantages, but dealing with the rush hour traffic in the city isn't one of them.

And as we're both very aware, when you become part of the force, the word 'late' is deleted from your vocabulary.

"Come on, baby, hurry up and get ready, then we can grab a quick bite to eat somewhere before I drop you at the base. This is going to be a long day for both of us and we don't want to start it late, right?"

"What are you going to do all these days without me?" I ask, caressing his taut skin along the bold lines of his shoulder tattoo. He's so strong, so fierce. So mine.

This is the first time we'll have been apart for more than a work day and it will be struggle.

A big one.

"Something will come to my mind," he murmurs before kissing my lips.

An hour later I've received the orders from my instructor and I'm in front of the USS Milius, the destroyer assigned to Vargas and me wondering why the name of the vessel is so fucking familiar.

I'm ready to walk up the narrow gang plank like someone condemned and about to be devoured by sharks.

Before you can achieve, you have to believe.

I believe I can, so I will. *A necessary reminder.*

"Okay, Zanetti," Vargas says. "We need to hurry up." He walks in front of me as he outranks me by tenure, only by a couple of weeks, but still.

My partner is far from a gentleman, I'm fully aware that he's lazy and intends to use my knowledge to make himself look good in order to progress his career. This weekend is going to be a nightmare, and I need to keep my wits in order to be two steps ahead of him.

A chief is waiting for our arrival and formally greets us, then hands us a clipboard with our orders.

"The captain is waiting for you at the stern, with some of the crew," he tells us.

There are about two hundred sailors standing on the deck in perfect formation, all neatly dressed in their work uniforms and lustrous black boots. My gaze wanders over dozens of unknown faces, feeling like the condemned contemplating a firing squad.

Until...

"Welcome, officers," a deep voice announces.

Damn man. Of course it had to be him.

Making a gigantic effort to avoid glaring at him, I manage to restrain myself.

Vargas and I walk the distance to them at a steady pace, greetings are made, protocol is followed.

By the time we're done, I want to throw myself overboard, this is going to be a nightmare. I can't concentrate working with him here.

"Good morning, Lieutenant Zanetti." That is supposed to be a formal greeting, but his tone is full of humor.

"You," I say accusingly. "Why you?"

"Did you honestly think I was going to let you go with anyone else?"

Adrik Houston is standing there in front of me with a smug expression and I can't quite believe it.

He knows how important this is to me, how much it has cost to get rid of the stigma of being the daughter of... Now, I have simply become the girlfriend of... My case goes from bad to worse.

Is this how my life is going to be, trapped with stubborn men who can't stand not getting their way, or have another rooster come to roam their chicken coop?

I want to kill him, I really do. I get that he's possessive. Come on, it's Commander Thunder, what else could I expect from him?

But this is different.

This is my career at stake and he's putting it at risk.

"How fucking dare you?" I hiss at him.

This is not happening, and soon as we are alone, I'll be spelling it out to him. However, before I can go for his jugular, he pulls rank.

"Are you ready to start work?" He quirks an arrogant eyebrow.

"I'm always ready, *sir,*" I answer haughtily.

"Lieutenant Zanetti, from the moment you set foot on my ship I became your captain, so forget that I'm your partner. You are under my command and you will comply with the orders I give you, no matter how difficult they are or whether or not you want to do it. I say jump and you will ask how high. Is that clear?"

I want to erase that smug smile from his face with my bare fists.

"Having fun?"

"I asked if that's clear, Lieutenant?"

Well, I can be professional, that's what I'm trained for after all.

"Crystal clear, sir," I answer, bringing my hand to my forehead.

"We're about to sail," he informs me. "I want a full report of the armament on board. Do you have the complete list?"

"Yes, sir," I answer formally. "Do you want to check it now?"

"Ladies first," he says, holding out his hand. "Go ahead."

This is nothing more than another test, among the many things we've had to memorize is the general layout of boats like this. There are currently several types of destroyers, and this one, the DDG-69, is classified as Arleigh Burke and belongs to the twenty-first squad.

We walk along a maze of corridors, then after going down a steep staircase, we arrive in the depths of the ship where the armaments are stored. I retrieve a list from my leather briefcase and we begin our review point by point.

To give him his due, Adrik is thorough, he asks a thousand questions, but after weeks of preparation, I can answer without any trouble, despite dying of nerves.

"You shared the preparation work with Lieutenant Vargas, Zanetti?"

"No, sir. Vargas is lazy, I preferred to do my homework without asking what his plans were."

"Wrong answer, Lieutenant." He reprimands me as if he doesn't know how much work I've put into this. "This is not an individual sport, teamwork is essential here. There is no place to hang individual glories. To survive war you must trust your partner, and learn to divide responsibilities. Otherwise, what would you intend to do, take the helm while at the same time taking care of the engine room?" When you are commander of a boat like this, you must delegate certain functions to the sailors in charge.

Shit, I didn't think about that.

My only priority was that everything went well, not worrying about making use of the douche assigned to me as a co-worker.

"The motto of this ship is 'Others before me'. Keep that in mind, Lieutenant, very much in mind."

"Can I speak freely, sir?"

"Go ahead," he authorizes.

"Sir, often Lieutenant Vargas *forgets* to do his job, to the point where he's lagging way behind the rest of us taking the course, although he wouldn't agree. I was afraid that if I waited for him to complete his part of the planning, we could run out of fuel in the middle of the exercise."

"Then it is your duty to inform the unit commander so that he can take charge of the situation," he lectures.

"What happens if I'm commanding the vessel and one of my fellow officers fails?"

"Then, Lieutenant, you must continue to follow the correct procedure. Always follow the chain of command, I've told you about that so many times."

Oh yes. Chain of command. If we survive this weekend without killing each other, I'm still going to strangle him as soon as we get home.

The way I've decided to organize everything down here is quite radical. I explain that, with my experience in new technologies, my main interest is to improve the conditions we're currently experiencing while using the minimum resources. These are hard times, and despite the large budget allocated to the militia in order to protect the country, every penny still counts.

I'm proud of the way he pays attention to my words. I know he's not doing it as the man in love with me, who shares his life with me. Here, he's my captain, my superior officer and, to make matters worse, the one in charge of evaluating my abilities as a future leader.

But more than that, I'm so fucking proud of what he's achieved. He started his career as an enlisted sailor, now he's a skipper. A commander—acting as captain of a vessel. Such an honor.

"Did you also organize the kitchen supplies?" Adrik asks when we're done and we head back up the stairs.

"No, sir, that's been done by Lieutenant Vargas, at least he completed that part of his work. An officer I admire told me once that food and fuel is vital for any mission."

The memory makes him smile. Our first night working together at my old apartment.

"You do know that alcoholic beverages are not allowed on board?"

"Sir, Vargas might be an immature douchebag, but I think even he is aware of how serious it would be to commit that kind of error."

"It reassures me to know that, Lieutenant."

He asks me to lead the way back to the bridge.

"Do you have the coordinates?" He wants to know when we reach our destination, and after I answer in the affirmative, he asks me to set the course.

I give the instructions, and so we set out toward the open sea, leaving behind the naval base and the normality of our life.

This is now a vessel ready for war.

Two days later I am about to climb the walls. We've not had time to sleep, having been woken up twice to carry out rescue drills.

I've had to repeat my mantra many times.

I believe I can, so I will.

It's become like a broken record in my head. This experience is like survival training, as officers we need to always be prepared and ready for combat. We sailors are forged by the sea and it isn't a merciful teacher.

Aside from that, I miss my boyfriend. He's long gone, instead I'm left with Commander Thunder in all his magnificence. What he told me is true, he's tough and demanding, but everything works like well-oiled machinery, the crew has a lot of respect for him and don't hesitate to obey his orders.

"Vargas," I shout to my colleague, trying to make myself heard above the wind and rain. "What are you supposed to be doing?"

The idiot is busy walking round a lifeboat inspecting it, instead of securing the helicopter that's just arrived. Basic rule, first things first, and with the waves we're facing right now, we must give priority to the equipment.

The lifeboat can wait since we checked it after the mission we carried out yesterday. Everything was in order then, so what could have changed in a few hours?

"Take care of your own business, Zanetti," he shouts back. "I'm busy here."

This surpasses even his usual idiocy, how can he not see where our priority should be?

"Smith, Mendez, Coleman," I call three of the men working with him, who immediately make themselves free to work with me. "Help me to secure the chopper with those chains over there."

"They can't do that until they've finished what they are doing here," Vargas shouts.

"Do you really need seven people to inspect a fifteen feet long boat? Don't fuck with me, Vargas."

"That's my problem, not yours," he replies.

"Well, when this multi-thousand-dollar helicopter goes overboard, it'll be you who has to do the explaining."

The men start sniggering as they watch us arguing.

"What, you think just because you're the daughter of the famous admiral Zanetti, you're always right?" Vargas taunts. "Think about it, you stupid woman. Even if you have been fast-tracked and given a promotion you don't deserve, you can't have everything handed to you on a silver platter."

"What the fuck is going on here?" a voice that I know very well demands to know.

"Sir, Vargas and I were arguing about…"

"Enough," he cuts me off before I can say another word.

"Vargas, in my office," he orders. "Now. Move!"

The poor bastard has no choice but to walk away with his tail between his legs once again.

"Lieutenant, take care of the helicopter and leave two men to check the lifeboat."

My expression can't hide the satisfaction I feel that someone has silenced that asshole.

"You can wipe that smile off your face. Even if what he did was wrong, you didn't act appropriately either," he says in a low voice.

"Sir? I don't understand what you mean."

"Do you think arguing in front of the crew that you are meant to be in charge of is any way to solve a difference between officers? You might both have the same rank, but Vargas has seniority over you."

"But Captain, the thing is…" I begin to explain, but he cuts me off again.

"Have I asked for any further explanation?"

His look makes it very clear that he is not waiting for an answer.

"In any case, I have to go and attend to matters. Carry on, Zanetti."

Yeah, yeah, I got it.

I am about to explode, so lend me one of the ropes attached to the helicopter so I can hang him from the first pole I find.

I mutter an answer and without further ado, he leaves me standing there in a rage.

"Lieutenant Zanetti," one of the chief of staff calls me later when I'm in the bow, waiting for the helicopter to be fueled again. "Commander Houston is waiting for you in his office."

"I'll be there shortly," I answer before making sure they finish the job and everything is as it should be.

Let's see what awaits me now.

I know where Adrik's small office is located, but this is the first time I've been here. I knock at the door and wait to be invited to enter.

"Come in."

He is standing in front of his desk waiting for me, arms crossed over his broad chest.

"God, I've missed you," he says as soon as I close the door behind me, coming to hover over my body.

"Don't you dare put your hands on me, asshole."

He freezes as he takes in my angry state, staring at me with bright smoky eyes, as if this is just a game to him.

"You want to fight with me?" he murmurs, taking my hand to put it over the erection hidden by his blue camouflaged pants. "Fine. Take your temper out on me. Let me take you over the desk, babe, we can have a death match."

"In your dreams," I answer, trying to push him away.

Adrik lets go of my hand, but my escape is short-lived as he focuses instead on the belt that I wear with my work pants.

"Let me go!" I spit out.

He might be strong, but I'm ready to fight him.

No, naughty mind. Not like that.

Not in the way he's expecting.

"Jordania, I've been wanting to do this for two days. Be thankful I didn't order you straight to my quarters and strip you when you first appeared on the deck of my ship."

"Well, it's good that you managed to control yourself, *sir*, and I'm sure than you can keep doing so. If there's nothing else, I will retire." I turn around, ready to open the door, but I didn't count on his agile reflexes preventing me.

"Oh, we're not done yet," he warns, beginning to unwind the camisole that I always wear under my uniform.

"Let me go," I protest, but my body betrays me by rubbing against him.

Against his hardness.

"Do you know how much I want you?" he hisses in my ear, making me shiver. "How much I love you?"

"Is that why you embarrassed me in front of the crew? Don't fuck with me, *Thunder*," I growl, almost spitting his nickname. I know how much it irritates him.

"But I am going to fuck you, babe, and for the record, just the way you like it," he replies. "Now, with reference to what happened on deck, I had to do it. Your attitude was unprofessional, and no matter how Vargas acted, that was not the way to proceed."

"But he was..." I argue.

"I've already taken care of him."

His explanation placates me, but not enough for me to yield. At least not yet.

"You should never disrespect another officer in front of the crew, Jordania. It causes them to lose respect and in the end that erodes the chain of command."

When he explains it that way, I guess my behavior wasn't exactly flawless.

"Okay, but what about you? Because when you finished with Vargas, you did exactly the same thing to me, you humiliated me."

"No," he answers, lowering the zipper of my pants. "It wasn't the same and you know it. I didn't make a big deal, I just spoke quietly to you. The men nearby might speculate about what I said to you, but in no way did I contradict you or humiliate you in front of them. I'd cut off my nuts before I'd ever do that."

His warm hand is caressing my folds through the cotton of my black panties.

"Do you want me to lend you my knife?"

I'm not going to surrender yet, I'll continue to fight this to the end.

"This is one of the reasons I love you so much, Jordania," he growls, as his fingers search between my legs.

"You're a fighter, so combative you're like the Valkyrie. That's why you've got me so crazy for you. My woman."

"The woman who will make you a eunuch at the first opportunity she has."

The damn man has the nerve to laugh, in fact he's cracking up.

"What, now I've become your private clown?"

"Listen to me," he says, turning me around in his arms. "Make sure you get this into that stubborn head of yours. I will never mock you, because you are mine, and I will always show you the respect you deserve. You will always be my top priority. Always."

I feel the cold edge of the desk against my butt and instinctively grab it. Adrik drops to his knees in front of me.

"This is my place, kneeling in front of you, worshiping my goddess." He looks up at me as he says this, and I'm unable to tear my eyes away from his.

He leans forward and begins to worship me, his tongue finding the hot, wet place that so eagerly awaits him.

This was what I needed. Although I'm still furious with him, I have also missed him.

End of statement.

Privacy now required.

Rule # 18: Danger is always around the corner for those who have something to hide.

Chapter
EIGHTEEN

"I'm so fucking proud of you," Adrik says as he closes the door to his office, then backs me up against the grey cold metal of his desk. "You did it, babe!"

His face is so serious, his gaze so intense he's burning my skin.

He kisses me and I forget even my name.

Adrik touches me with skills I can't understand, I'm really tired, but my body is buzzing with excitement. It's a strange feeling my brain can't comprehend, it's fueled by instinct, and makes the entire vessel fade away. He's a live wire, and I'm standing in deep waters, ready to be electrified.

He's thunder and storm. And all mine.

I know he's as tired as I am. He supervised each exercise, sometimes from the bridge, other times directly from the deck but his presence was everywhere, billowing around like a heavy fog. It's one of the reasons his vessel works like a well-greased machine.

"I hope you won't be congratulating Vargas this way, sir." My hands caress the nape of his neck, playing with the short strands of his dark hair, while he holds my face in his hands, caging me.

As if I'd want to be anywhere else.

"I will be speaking to Captain Nolan about Vargas since he's…" He stops himself. He shouldn't be discussing how Vargas performed with me, that would be a serious breach of protocol. We're both aware that the line separating the two sides of our lives is blurring, and it's a difficult balance to maintain.

"Are you coming home with me?" I ask, changing the subject.

He needs sleep as much as I do, but as he lets out a deep sigh, I know I won't like his reply.

"Here are my keys, you know where I parked the truck." The cold metal feels heavy in my hand. I don't want to leave without him, but I understand duty calls. "I should be home in time to have dinner with you."

He might be speaking the words, but his body is saying something else, given the huge erection I can feel standing to attention, ready and waiting for his marching orders to go to war in the naked world.

Fuck, it's barely noon. Dinner sounds too far away.

On the bright side, it gives me time to fix something lovely for us, maybe a little picnic on our third floor terrace since the weather is amazing. I'm already planning something spicy and I'm not talking about naughty lingerie. I'm thinking of Adrik's favorite Mexican food and some beers, then heading back to our bed for some much needed sleep for both of us.

With a heavy heart, we part ways. He must remain on board to review some paperwork, which I think means he's going to evaluate our performances. Outside his office walls, Adrik has been totally and utterly professional, being the committed leader he is. I've been in awe of him, seeing the way he commands his vessel.

The entire crew has been eager to follow his orders, there've been no mistakes thanks to his clear and concise orders. The entire operation was a well-planned and rehearsed maneuver, making my admiration for him grow even more.

Some might say I'm seeing things through rose tinted glasses, but that's not the case. Watching Adrik commanding his vessel was a magnificent performance that would have impressed anyone.

I also met Carter Glasgow, one of his lieutenants, and I also got to work with Zephyr Herrera, one of Adrik's best friends, who I met before when he came over the house to have dinner. He's a funny guy, a bit immature in my opinion, but who am I to judge? Zeph is Chase's—my friend Roselynn's husband—cousin.

Never in my life have I been so happy to see mainland again, and when I disembark, I almost kiss the ground. I feel dirty and stinky, although my assigned cabin had a private shower, time was very limited. So now all I need is a long hot bath, a bottle of wine—or two—and a good twelve solid hours of uninterrupted sleep, preferably wrapped up in my man's strong arms.

From the bottom of my handbag, I hear my cell phone ringing, and I hurry to answer, crossing my fingers, hoping it's Adrik telling me to wait so we can go home together.

I let out a big disappointed sigh when I see it's my father calling.

Who else would pick that moment to call?

"Jordan, apparently you're already on land," he says by way of greeting.

"Yes, sir. Since five minutes ago," I reply in a weary voice, emulating his attitude, like a chip off the old block.

"I'm here in San Diego and looking forward to seeing you in your apartment in an hour, Lieutenant."

Goodbye to my long bath and my well-deserved hours of rest. Crap. Here we go, if he hasn't already heard, he will now.

"I haven't been living in the assigned accommodation for weeks now. I'm living in a beautiful house in downtown."

"What? Did you buy a house without telling me first?"

I can already tell he's going to be difficult. Guess it's in the genes.

"Dad, I've called you so many times. I tried to invite you to our Christmas brunch. I left a thousand messages with your secretary."

"I've been busy. There's so much to do, but I did send you a Christmas gift."

Yeah, I know. A solitaire diamond hung on a fine platinum chain. Sure, it was beautiful, but I missed having my father there with me. I fell in love with Adrik's family, they were so sweet and welcomed me with open arms, but there's an empty spot in my heart. Every time I see a vacant chair at the table, my heart aches missing my own family.

The family I've never had.

"Dad, I wanted you to meet Adrik since we're living together, and you're…"

"Why the hell are you doing that?" he replies angrily. "Why are you living with Houston?"

"Because it's my life and I wanted to be with him. You may not like it, but I'm an adult and I have the right to make my own decisions."

I hear him sigh on the other end of the line, obviously struggling to keep his patience.

"I'll call you back in half an hour when I've arranged somewhere for us to meet. Make sure you're ready."

He hangs up before I can even say goodbye. Feeling depressed and weary, I go home to take a shower and get ready. Half an hour later, my father calls me again with his usual military precision.

Resigned to meeting up with him, I wear one of those wide leg pants with a fancy blouse and high heels, taking special care over my appearance as a form of armor, not wanting to appear weak or vulnerable.

"Come in and sit down," my father orders as soon as I enter the office he got for us to meet in.

Not a kiss, not a hug, no sign of affection from him whatsoever.

Where is the father who told me before I boarded that plane in Pearl Harbor that my happiness was the most important thing to him?

Now I understand why I lack any maternal instinct. With the example he sets, it's a miracle I'm not carved from ice.

"What are you doing living with a son of a bitch like Houston?" my father angrily demands.

Where is this shit coming from?

Why does he refer to Adrik in those terms?

I don't care what he thinks, it doesn't matter. What I know and believe to be true is all that matters.

And Adrik Houston is the man I love.

The man I have decided to share both my present and my future with.

"Adrik is an honorable man, one of the best commissioning officers I've known. He has an impeccable career and a bright future. You should be pleased for me."

He looks at me, his dark eyes tired and worried. This is new.

"I'm not talking about his career, that bastard has the connections, the achievements, the awards. He's on the path to be Chairman of the Joint Chiefs of Staff. But I'm not talking about his awards as an officer. I'm talking about his honor as a man."

What the fuck is my father talking about?

"I'm an adult, and as such I don't have to give you any explanations concerning my private life. While I was living under your roof I complied with your rules, but now I pay my own debts and expenses, and how I choose to live my private life is none of your business."

It never should have been, so now I'm putting a stop to it. I am no longer a little girl.

There it is, the truth has to be told.

"But what about your career?" he demands, clearly exasperated. "Your future?"

"It's precisely because I'm thinking about those things that I'm with him. I know that Adrik is a man that I'm proud to be with. If you don't like it, then that's your problem, not mine."

"I had plans for you, Jordania Marie."

"Can't you see that I don't care about the map you had drafted out for my life? I'm not stupid and I'm perfectly capable of making my own choices."

My father's face is almost purple, he isn't used to being defied. He's used to having the last word, but we're cut from the same cloth, and as his offspring, I've inherited many of his traits.

I don't know much about my mother, I've no idea what made her tick, but I miss her every time we clash, wishing she were here, smoothing things out, mediating between us.

"Don't provoke me," he warns.

"Sir, if you have no other business to deal with, I ask for your permission to…" I say, rising from my chair.

"Permission denied," he orders. "Sit down, shut up, and listen to me. In that order, Jordania."

"You can talk all you want, but I'll decide if I'm going to listen."

My father paces around, breathing hard.

"Just hold your tongue," he says, "because I'm about to lose my temper. I've come a long way to see you."

Oh no, he's not playing the old-man-traveling card, I'm not going to feel guilty or sorry for him.

"Yeah, well if you wanted to know more about my whereabouts, there's this amazing gadget called a cell phone. Oh but wait, you do have one because you used it to call me today, in fact I'm sure you use it all the time. But if you had bothered to keep in touch, you might have met my boyfriend before and even had a civilized conversation with us. You know, we missed you at Christmas, his family was there with us and…"

"That's irrelevant."

Why is he being like this?

"If this is about the argument we had regarding my previous relationship, you can forget it. I don't have to justify my actions, that was a private matter between the two of us."

"This isn't about that, I haven't spoken to Sanders in a long time and you know it. I'm here to find out what the hell you're doing with a man like Houston!"

I'm so over this, and so tired of arguing with my father.

"If you want me to explain the nature of my relationship with Adrik Houston, you're wasting your time. I suggest you find something else to entertain yourself with while you're in town."

Eyes as dark as mine glare at me. My father is not the type of person who is easily intimidated but neither am I, we both know that. Clearly furious, he walks over to the desk, grabs a manila envelope from the drawer and puts it in my trembling hands.

"Then please can you explain how these images reached my hands?"

Not understanding a word of what my father is saying, I open the yellow envelope, and pull out a series of black and white photographs.

The shock of what I'm seeing steals my ability to breathe. I can't even think straight.

Thanks to these eight by ten prints, I'm transported to an alternate world where my life has become a low budget movie. In the middle of the blurry shadows the identity of the characters is quite clear.

This can't be happening. This is a nightmare, a horrible vicious nightmare that threatens to turn my life into shambles.

It's him.

It's me.

Jesus Christ!

What the hell is this all about?

Where did these pictures come from?

And who would send them to my father?

Rule # 19: The most important battle is the one in which you fight for her.

Chapter NINETEEN

My father's cold hands rest on my shoulders while I carefully study each of the photographs he has given me.

My hands are shaking and I'm struggling to breathe normally. I should say something, but the words stick to my throat.

Bodies twisting together, sweating. Mouths open, screaming with pleasure.

There's no doubt that it's us, Adrik and me. In my bed. When we met on the stairs, the first night we had dinner together. There are at least thirty images. Some are from my accident after our shopping expedition, not in the parking lot, but from when we got back, pictures of me crying with a bruised face standing outside our door, then some of us arguing.

They paint a terrible picture. These images have been carefully chosen to make a big impact on my father.

I can't even blink, this is such a low blow. One that, without a doubt, I never expected.

"He hit you," my father states.

"It was an accident," I try to explain, but as soon as the words leave my mouth I realize my mistake. I sound just like those abused women who defend their partners using the exact same excuse.

But this time it's the truth.

"I tripped and fell." What else can I say? I'm not lying. "Adrik was worried sick, he drove me straight to the hospital. I had a sprained ankle and a huge bruise on my face."

My father's face turns angrier by the second, each word only adding fuel to the flame burning inside him.

"And these?" He points to the pictures taken on the stairs. I can't deny they look really bad taken out of context like this, they make it seems as if Adrik is abusing me.

Frustration, shame and, above all, anger, begin to swirl in my chest. Forging a storm that is about to explode.

My eyes fill with tears, although they are not sad tears, I'm way too angry for that.

And no way am I going to collapse in front of my father. I will stay strong.

I will not allow him to browbeat me when I know for a fact this is not what it seems.

I was there. He was not.

"Where did these come from?" I try to keep my temper in check and stick to factual questions, in an attempt to work out what the hell is going on.

"Someone left the envelope in the mailbox outside my office," he informs me.

"You must have some idea who the fuck sent you this shit?" I state.

"Does that matter?"

"Of course it matters, I want to know everything, everything," I yell in frustration, losing the battle to keep my cool. "Are you listening to me? Everything."

My father takes a couple of steps back, moving away from where I'm still sitting.

"The truth is that I don't know," he admits. "The envelope was hand-delivered, not mailed to me, and of course there was no sender written on it, no mail stamp. Nothing."

"I don't understand who the fuck could have taken these pictures. But naturally you jump to conclusions and assume the worst, that Adrik plans to blackmail me to further his career and, as if that wasn't bad enough, also abusing me."

"Jordan, clearly those photos were taken from inside the room, so who else could it be but Houston? I think someone, maybe one of his accomplices, decided to do the right thing and play the same game the bastard is playing with you."

"I find it unbelievable and highly improbable," I state, unwilling to even consider that Adrik would act in that way.

Adrik loves me, I'm sure he does. I can't believe that a man who pursued me with such utter determination would do this shit. Because that's what this is. Horseshit. Someone has it in for us, for our relationship.

Someone who knows me well. Someone who knows how important my name is to me. How important my career is. My reputation.

In the military, reputation is everything.

Everything.

"Check it out for yourself."

I turn my attention to the images I still have on my lap. With a heavy heart and raging mind, I go through them all, one by one. What my father says is true, they've been taken from inside my room and from the same angle.

Whoever took them must have concealed a camera in that room, somewhere I'd never discover it.

The question remains the same. *Who?*

I don't know if it's something to be thankful for, but fortunately none of the pictures show me completely naked. The image quality is very low, although it's perfectly clear that it's me. In one of them you can only see my back while I'm lying on top of Adrik.

In another, you can see my ecstatic expression as he holds me in his arms, sitting on the bed. They're that kind of photos.

This is a nightmare, it has to be.

Please, someone pinch me and wake me up.

Right now!

Please?

"I have to talk to Adrik," I murmur, completely bewildered.

"There's nothing to say to that man, nothing he can say to excuse any of this. While I was flying across the country, one of the best lawyers in the force drafted some paperwork for you to sign, an affidavit which will support the criminal complaint. I'm taking the motherfucker to court. He messed with the wrong family."

"Complaint? *The wrong family?*"

What is this all about?

"I'm not underage and it definitely wasn't rape or any kind of abuse. Yes, I had an accident before Christmas, but shit like that happens when there are careless teenagers with skates around. I'm not signing anything and you can't force me."

"This is disclosure of private events, in which an officer has been involved. You were not aware of this, it is dishonorable conduct, Jordan. Enough reason to take him to court to be dishonorably discharged."

"I have to talk to him, Dad. Adrik will be arriving at our home soon, he's still at work right now."

"That place is not your home," he insists. "And stop saying you're going to talk to that bastard, he lost that right when he treated you so despicably. If it were up to me, I'd order his arrest right now, but there are procedures that have to be followed."

"I don't care what you say, this is my problem and I have to be the one to solve it."

I hastily shove the photos back in the envelope they arrived in.

Adrik has to see them.

I try to get up, pushing on the arms of the chair, but my father leans down to prevent me.

"It became my problem the moment that envelope came into my hands," he growls. "You are going to sit there and listen to everything I have to say. Then you are going to put your signature on the document, and then we will take care of Houston."

"No, that's not happening," I cry, not caring if my voice is heard outside the office. "This is a personal matter."

"Wake up, Jordania Marie, open your eyes," he yells back. "Right now anyone could receive those images by email. It's not only your name that's at stake here, but it's also *my name. The family name.*"

"That's what this is really all about, isn't it?" I accuse him. "Well, you can keep your precious name since it means so much to you. Las Vegas is only four hours from here, so maybe I'll just get married and swap it for something less inconvenient for you."

I'm lashing out, but if I were a man, right now my father would be squeezing my balls and, that's not something I can allow.

He doesn't care about my career, or the pain this situation is causing me, all he wants is to remain untainted, worried about how it will affect him if a scandal breaks out.

"I'm going to call Casper Sewell, he's still your friend, isn't he?" he states with the authority of one accustomed to giving orders. "He'll help me convince you, get you to see reason. I don't understand why he didn't warn me, then all this crap could have been avoided. You, my only daughter, involved with a worthless nobody like Houston. Jordan, you have really disappointed me, I expected more from you."

His words are like a dagger to the heart. I'm not lying. The knife has been there for years, but with every word, it twists deeper, causing the wound to bleed.

"You don't need to call Casper," I say, getting up from my chair. I'm out of here.

My voice is as determined as my actions, he's not going to stop me.

"Jordan," he says.

"No, Dad," I answer. "This isn't between you and me. You can try and order me to stop, but you know I won't. Try tying me to the chair, I'll just scream bloody murder, I'll bring the walls down. If you want to avoid a scandal, you'll let me out of this office to handle this situation in my own way."

"Do you have any brains in your head?" he says when he realizes I'm serious. "Doesn't matter, I can handle this without you. As soon as internal affairs finds out and takes action on the matter, his career will be over. He'll be out of the force, no pension, nothing."

But I can be as stubborn as my father. I am blood of his blood and when a Zanetti gets something in their head, the world better be prepared.

I lift my chin and our eyes meet. In his, I see the frustrated anger of someone who is powerless, and in mine, he must see how determined I am to do this my way.

I believe I can… I'll fight for myself, and I'll fight for him too.

I leave the office, closing the door softly behind me. Ignoring the looks that some people throw my way, I continue walking tall, with my head held high.

But inside I am breaking apart.

I need time to think. I need to figure out how to get to the nitty gritty of this fucking mess. A good place to start? Home. I really need to talk this through with Adrik. Together we'll clean up this shit.

Together we are powerful.

The drive home is quiet, I don't turn on the radio and the breeze on my face from the open window helps to clear my head. Who the fuck could be so twisted and jealous of us to do something so spiteful?

Who?

The silence at home is welcome, and as soon as I close the door behind me, the heaviness of this fucking mess hits me hard, right in the chest. Tears cascade down my cheeks and there is nothing I can do to stop them.

I need an outlet before I explode. I'm here alone, I can allow myself a pause, to be weak for a couple of minutes and think.

And to mourn.

I cry for myself and for what is happening, I cry for my father and how he acted. I also cry for Adrik and for what is about to happen to him, because knowing Admiral Zanetti the way I do, I know he will not be stopped so easily.

What is the solution to this mess?

How can we solve it and get out of this wasp's nest?

Wow, I've been generous, this is the apocalypse, with the four horsemen and everything.

In these past few months Adrik has become not only the man I love, but my favorite place in the entire world. He has become my family, my rock. My everything.

He's the vessel in this war called life, and I'm ready to fight.

For me and for him. For us.

I refuse to believe that the man who told me he loves me is the brain behind this horrific scheme, I refuse. Something deep down tells me I'm right, that my instincts about him are not wrong. Some would argue it's just my heart speaking, but I just know that's not the case.

I'm panicking, afraid of what I may lose, of what is at stake here.

And it's not just about my career. I fear for the both of us. At the center of the whirlwind of questions that are tormenting my head, two questions are constantly on repeat. Who? And why?

I stand and walk to the dining room, the gray shadowy wall seems an omen for my immediate future, a stark reminder. There are a lot of dark clouds looming over us.

But I'm ready. He's thunder, I'm lightning.

Might and strength.

I take the pictures out of the envelope to take another look. I need to find the source, because all the images were taken from the same point. But where? My old bedroom was sparsely furnished. There were no pictures hanging on the wall, no stuffed animals where a camera could be concealed.

When Adrik finally comes through the door, I'm still there, standing by the table looking at the pictures with an overhead lamp as if I'm studying a complicated navigation map. I've been looking at them for a while, trying to find a clue in the shadows.

"Jordania, babe?" he calls out, before appearing in my field of vision still wearing his camo.

He stands in front of me, silently taking in everything around me.

"What the hell is all of this?" he asks, reaching down to take one of the photographs, then his face contorts in disgust.

Welcome to the club. He's about to be as mad as I am.

"Babe, where did you get these photos?" he angrily demands, tension emanating from his strong body. "Where did these come from?"

He stands there looking at me, while I'm unable to explain.

"I don't know," I murmur, when I finally find my voice.

"You're going to have to give me more than that," he says in a deceptively quiet voice, which I find scarier than if he'd shouted. "Jordania, where did you get these photos?"

"My father handed them to me a short while ago," I finally answer.

"Who gave them to him?" He continues with his interrogation, the implacable officer taking charge of the situation. Good, because right now I need someone to lean on.

Today more than ever.

"I don't know, Adrik, I just don't know," I whisper, almost choking on every word. Increasingly weaker, more tired. "My father is furious, he wants to prosecute you, get you discharged from the force."

And suddenly I know for certain. It hits me like an avalanche. What I feel for him is true love, because I care more about his welfare and safety than I do for my own.

"I don't care about what happens to me!" His angry voice shakes me up, and at the same time puts me back together.

But he needs to know about my father's plans, we need to work out a strategy, a war ploy.

"He had some paperwork he wanted me to sign, accusing you of disclosure of private facts and improper conduct against an officer. Adrik, my father said that he is going to end you, one way or another."

He stares at me, those smoky eyes almost incandescent in the light of our home as the muscles in his neck tense.

"Jordania, this not only affects me, it will have a big impact on you as well, you must know that."

I shrug, downplaying the matter.

No doubt my father will ensure I'm portrayed as a victim, a foolish woman who allowed herself to be exploited. Then I'll be relegated to a dark corner in a little office somewhere in a Godforsaken building, treated like someone with a contagious disease.

I will have lost my honor and in the military, that's a fate worse than death.

"What difference does that make?" I sigh.

"This isn't going to happen like that, I'm not going to allow it," he insists.

He puts one of the photographs in his uniform pocket and gets up, then looks for something in the kitchen, before leaving the house slamming the door, leaving me there, alone and without comfort, because dealing with the object of his anger is more important right now.

I'd don't want to be the target of Adrik's anger. He's like a huge boiler, the fire has been lit, and now there's no limit to the power unleashed.

I almost feel sorry for the person behind this mess. *Almost.*

Rule # 20: Fight for what you really want. The path to success is not an easy one, and is for those who never give up.

Chapter
TWENTY

Adrik

I've never considered myself a lucky man. That shit doesn't exist as far as I'm concerned. You make your own luck, it's what you carve out for yourself, what you achieve by sweating your ass off.

Even so, many would say that I have been lucky, but that's not true. I don't care if they call me arrogant, but I know how hard I've had to work to get to where I am, and it has made me who I am today.

Chance? Not at all. I figured out pretty early on there were only two paths I could choose from.

I could be someone who worked hard to achieve their goals and better themselves, or I could give up, drift along, and get sucked into all kinds of trouble and end up locked up in a cell for life.

For me it was a no-brainer. I stepped up, faced the hard reality that is life, and worked hard to become a decent man. My nature has always been restless and impatient, but I was bright and observant. Growing up, my best friend and I might have been dealt a shitty hand of cards, but we were both determined to make something of ourselves. It was great having an accomplice, someone who also desperately wanted to find the green shoots amongst the rubble.

Many teenagers are rebellious growing up, but that was not the case with me. Although I had a lot of energy to burn, I tried to follow the example my grandparents had set for me. Putting in hard work is the only way to climb the ladder. If you wait for everything to fall into place, then you'll die waiting without a penny to your name.

I owe my grandparents everything, and I wanted to repay them. That was the main reason I enlisted, as a means to earn a decent living and ensure a good retirement for them, since they gave me the priceless gift of a happy childhood. They took care of me, nurtured me, and gave me a very loving, affectionate, and close family. Without them, I don't know what would have become of me, since my father was—and still is—a sad piece of shit, and I never knew my mother. Her name might be on my birth certificate, but other than that I know nothing about her, and she has never attempted to make contact.

There was nothing sad about my childhood, I grew up in a normal household, with two loving people taking care of me, even when they had to count the pennies to buy me a new pair of shoes. Of course, kids can be cruel, and some made fun of me—or tried to—mocking my family situation, but I never, ever, felt ashamed of who I was. It only made me stronger, made me who I am today.

It gives me great comfort now that I can stand with my head held high, knowing that I've made my grandparents proud, and *I am proud* of how far I've come. I've worked my ass off to be the man I am today.

So, I've never considered that luck played any part in my life.

Until I met *her*, and everything changed. She was like a lightning bolt sent directly from heaven.

How could I resist her? It was impossible.

I'm not going to lie. It was her ass that first caught my attention. Firm and round, wiggling in front of my eyes, covered only by a small red striped bikini.

Too honest? No, I promise you this was something different. She was leaning over, ready to swing on a rope, and jump into the water.

Physically, I was certainly attracted to her like a moth to a flame, but there was something more.

With Jordania, I quickly discovered there was more.

I wanted to be with her in the light of day and do dirty things in the darkness of night.

I had fun teasing her with a few cheesy pick-up lines that made her smile, but instead of flirting back like a typical girl, she was prepared to fight the sizzling attraction shimmering between us, like the Valkyrie she is. I spent most of that day fighting the urge to take her in my arms to kiss her and enjoy her feistiness, her wit, her sassiness. She casted a magic spell, capturing me in her web but at the same time, setting me free.

It was exhilarating.

And then she threw out the dare, leaving our fate floating in the air.

But destiny brought us together again.

Coincidence? No, we were meant to be. Serendipity, my grandma would say. And for the first time in my life, I believed in destiny, in a force forging a path for me. The writing was on the wall, guiding me to her.

What are the odds of us meeting in the first place? Very low. Two strangers on a remote island.

Then after that, two officers stationed on the same base, at the same time. She was right there, within my grasp, and also off limits. Navy's golden girl. Admiral Bauer's daughter.

I wasn't going to be stupid enough to let her go a second time.

She was worth the chase. And all the risks.

That's what got me acting like a lovesick fool, determined to discover the person hidden behind the walls she put up to protect herself.

But I broke through.

Now, when she's afraid, I will be her rock. When she's cold, my arms will be there to warm her. When doubts threaten to drown her, I will become the air she needs to breathe.

I owe her everything, because she's given me everything I ever wanted or needed, a gift so precious, I would have never dared to imagine it for a nobody like me.

The first time I entered her body, I found a paradise that I never knew existed, and after that I'd do anything to get lost in the intensity of her dark eyes, and have that long, black hair fanning out on my pillow every night, her perfume lingering between the sheets.

She cast a spell on me, the way she calls out my name, welcoming me, asking me to kiss her, begging me to make love to her, all at once.

Sometimes, I have to keep my hands in my pockets to control the urge to touch her inappropriately. She has turned me into a teenager again with all the uncontrollable hormones. I'm surprised that at my last physical exam I wasn't diagnosed with Priapus disease, I'm in a constant state of arousal.

Jordania has a body made for sin and I'm going straight to hell.

But that's not all.

I have seen her fight tooth and nail to achieve her dream, never letting go of her goal. Many have tried to knock her back, discourage her, and now someone is trying to destroy her. But first they will have to go through me to get to her.

I don't give a damn about what this could cost me. I'm a man of simple tastes and although it could potentially mean selling the house I just bought, we will survive. I know people, I have contacts, so if it came to it, I could easily get another job. I'm certainly not afraid of getting my hands dirty to provide for my family. My grandfather taught me well. Any self-respecting man must remember the two P's.

Provide.

Protect.

I've been doing it ever since I became an adult, and I'm not about to change who I am now, certainly not with her by my side.

I've fought for my country and for the freedom of millions of people I don't even know. Now there is a bigger goal on my horizon.

Jordania Zanetti is worth fighting for. I would give every last drop of my blood to see her happy.

Happy and safe.

I have plans for the future with her, big plans. This disaster is not going to stop me from making them a reality. Soon she will have my ring on her finger and my last name embroidered on the pocket of her uniform.

Old-fashioned? When it comes to her, I'm a fucking caveman. No one messes with my woman and gets away with it.

I press the same number on the screen of my phone for the fifteenth time, cursing and swearing, trying to clear the lump in my throat I've had since finding her at home in a sea of tears.

I could have stayed to comfort Jordania, but it was more important to get all this crap sorted for her, even if my hands end up stained with the blood of whoever did this.

Because I plan to kill whoever it was with my own bare hands.

"Finally you answer the fucking phone," I say, when my call is eventually picked up.

"And hello to you too, Commander Thunder," he says mockingly. "Missing me already? I thought you had plans with your woman."

"Where the hell are you? I need you to come to the base immediately." I'm in no mood to deal with his stupid jokes.

"Is it important?" For fuck's sake, he knows it must be, otherwise I wouldn't be calling him.

"Zephyr, meet me at Jordania's old apartment, right *now*."

"Shit, Houston, I'm a bit busy right now," he grumbles, as I hear a girl laughing in the background.

"Damn, Zephyr, just for once, can you please just keep it in your pants? I need you here right the fuck now." One day his man-whoring ways are going to catch up with him.

When he realizes how serious I am, his attitude changes immediately, and I know he'll be here as soon as he can to help me clear up this shit show.

I take the picture I brought with me from my uniform pocket and start looking for the damn camera in Jordanias' almost empty room.

It takes me less than two minutes to find it hidden inside the air conditioning duct, and suddenly I feel like such an idiot, a poor naïve sucker. I can't believe that someone, using resources as basic and crude as this, has put us in such a mess. If I had been more careful, this would not be happening. But who would think of looking for hidden cameras or microphones, especially in a place like this? We're on a naval base, for fuck's sake.

The camera is a wireless device that connects to the network automatically, I've seen gadgets like this before. I'll make a couple of calls to see what I can find out. That's where having contacts is useful, especially in a situation as nasty as this.

I'm relieved when there's a knock on the door, the infantry has arrived. Zephyr will surely help me solve this crap and then I can get back home and take my woman to bed.

But when I open it, it's not my second in command.

"Commander Houston," says one of the men I find standing there. "Please join us, sir."

Wow, Admiral Zanetti must certainly have pulled every trick in the book to have moved so fast.

Zephyr arrives next, running down the corridor in civilian attire.

"Sir?"

"One second, please."

The petty officer nods, although he doesn't step back. I grab hold of Zeph, telling him the first thing that comes to mind. "Take care of Jordania."

Herrera knows what I mean, we've worked together long enough for him not to miss my meaning. Despite his obvious concern, he knows what to do next.

"I'll call Benson," he calls to me, as I'm escorted out by the three sailors, headed to the base command.

The preliminaries are over.

The war has just begun.

Rule # 21: A woman forgives, but never forgets. Think before doing or saying something that you might regret later.

Chapter
TWENTY-ONE

Some people are afraid of the dark, but right now I'm more afraid of the things waiting for me in the light.

Adrik left hours ago, and ever since I've been restlessly pacing around the table. I know I should trust him, I know the kind of man he is, but my mind is reeling. He hasn't returned, and with each passing minute, it feels as if I have a noose around my neck and it's getting tighter and tighter.

Some might wonder why I'm hanging around, others would say I'm a fool for blindly believing that he's not behind all this. The rest would think that if a man like my father says it's true, he must be right.

Am I being blind? Weak? Perhaps, but I'm letting my heart guide me. If they had seen with their own eyes the way he is with me, they would understand that Adrik, *my Adrik*, isn't involved in this shit.

No matter how hard I try, I can't think of a single reason why he would want to hurt me so much, not a single one.

Instead, he has told me many times that he loves me, that he really loves me. Words can flutter in the breeze, but actions speak louder. He has worked so hard to win my heart and continues to do so every day. With every smile, with every look, every time he takes my hand, I can feel that this connection is real, eternal, indestructible.

How could I turn my back on all of that?

How could I turn my back on my other half?

How could I turn my back on my beliefs and my faith?

I can't. I wouldn't be true to myself, and that's not something I'm willing to do, not even at a time like this. I have to trust my instincts.

I have to know the truth, get to the bottom of this shitfest. Knowledge is power, and right now I feel powerless standing here in the dark, both literally and figuratively.

I look down at my clothes, noticing for the first time how creased they are, thinking these wrinkled layers of fabric are a good analogy of what my life will be like after the scandal breaks, which I have no doubt won't take long. Even if I somehow manage to get through it, the stigma will remain, I'll carry the scars for life.

Is my attitude defeatist? Or am I just being realistic?

But before drowning in self-pity, I must first talk to Adrik. Something tells me that this attack isn't about me, it's an attack against *him*.

Someone is clearly after him, wants him out.

The question is, who?

There is a loud knock at the door and my first thought is that it must be Adrik, but then I realize it can't be him, he knows the lock's code, and at this time on a Sunday it won't be any of our friends or neighbors trying to break the door down. Whoever is outside is very insistent.

"Didi?" Casper calls from the other side of the door. "Didi, are you there?"

Before I can respond, the lock turns and the man who's been my best friend for years walks into the house I share with Adrik.

It doesn't take him long to find me, it's not like there's a lot of places to hide even though Adrik has furnished the house.

"What are you doing here?" I ask, once I get over the shock of seeing him.

"I came to see you, of course," he replies. "Your father called me, he's worried about you."

As we go into the house, I don't bother to turn on any lamps, but even in the sparse light I notice Casper turning his nose up as if my home is filthy or stinky.

"And no doubt he's furious too," I sigh.

"You know him well," he agrees, stuffing his hands deep in the pockets of his jeans. "Didi, what are you doing here? Why aren't you at least packing your stuff?"

He scowls as he glances around disapprovingly.

"I'm sorry?" *What does he mean, what is he talking about?*

I don't like where this conversation is heading, something isn't right here.

"Didi, I totally agree with your father, you need to get away from Houston immediately. Look at the mess that bastard has gotten you into, your career is going down the drain. Come on, I'll help you pack."

Casper grabs me by the arms, trying to force me up the stairs to the second floor. He's gripping me so hard he's hurting me, and a knot of apprehension hits my chest.

This is a runaway train heading off the tracks.

Jordania, keep calm. I repeat to myself over and over. I have to keep it together and think on my feet.

"It's fine, I can manage on my own," I say, trying to act as if I'm not worried by his odd behavior.

I've no intention of packing or going anywhere. "Do you need help packing?"

"No, because I'm not leaving, Casper," I say firmly.

"I can't believe you're in denial like this, don't you realize what's going on?"

The coldness of Casper's voice sends a shiver right through me.

"Casper, Adrik's done nothing wrong, none of this is his fault."

"Didn't you see the photos of you two together?" There it is again, something odd in his gaze that I don't recognize.

Casper runs his hands over his eyes before wiping them over his face in frustration.

"I know you're confused, Didi, but there can be no doubt," he insists, raising his voice. "It had to be him."

"I don't care what you say, I refuse to believe it."

Casper's knuckles turn white as he clenches his hands into tight fists. He's losing his composure along with his grip on reality.

"Didi, the photos were taken inside your room. What more proof do you want?"

"Are you telling me you've seen them?" I ask, horrified and embarrassed to think that my best friend has seen such intimate pictures of me, of us, of things that should only be between Adrik and me.

"No, no," he quickly backtracks, as he sees my horrified reaction. "Your father told me about them."

"Casper, don't you think that if Adrik really was behind all this, it would've been much easier for him to hide the camera in his room?" Even he has to concede that this is a fair point. "Wouldn't it have been easier in his apartment or even here?"

He hesitates before answering. "Well, I don't know, I've no idea what's going on in that degenerate's mind." While he's talking, I need to try and defuse this situation.

"I think you should go now, Adrik will be here soon, I'm just waiting for him to get back."

What I really want is to tell him to go away and leave me alone, because there's something going on here that's making me very uncomfortable. Maybe it's nothing, but why do I feel like I'm talking to a stranger and not my best friend? I need to talk to Adrik, and I need to start making some calls as soon as possible. I know a couple of lawyers and now that I've pulled myself together and stopped feeling sorry for myself, I must start organizing things.

Casper scratches his bald head as he paces around looking increasingly agitated and about to erupt.

"Didi, there are things you don't know about Houston."

"Like what?"

I'm getting so annoyed with him. I've tried to be diplomatic, but he has to stop interfering and trying to boss me around. Why can't he just go away and leave me alone? I have important things I need to get done.

Of course there are things I don't know about Adrik yet, it takes time to get to know everything, but what does Casper know that I don't?

"Your father opposed Houston's promotion and he almost succeeded. However, Houston used his connections, he's a sly fox who managed to persuade the right people in the right circles."

That has to be a lie, my father would certainly have mentioned it. And Adrik wouldn't have kept quiet, not about something so important.

But Casper? Why is he making these accusations?

What does he have to gain from this?

I don't want to think badly of my old friend, but he's making it hard not to.

My mood has changed, I'm ready to fight.

No war is ever won by giving up.

I am a warrior, a sailor. I've been forged by the sea.

Casper's expression hardens. He's up to something, I just don't know what.

"That fool won't be coming back here any time soon," he growls, anger masking his face. "They already arrested him, your father moved fast."

"Then I need to move faster." I run to find my phone. It's time to call in the reinforcements. Adrik needs me.

"Just forget about him, Jordan," Casper shouts as he grabs my arm to stop me.

"Let me go! What the hell do you think you're doing?" He's surprisingly strong considering how slim he is.

And suddenly all the pieces of this intricate puzzle fall into place, revealing the bigger picture.

"You will come with me," he threatens. "You have no choice."

I can't believe I've been so blind, so stupid.

"I will not!" I growl at him. "You'd better let me go before someone hears me screaming and thinks the worst."

"Really?" he asks, raising his eyebrows. "You want to make this worse? I'd think about it if I were you, Lieutenant."

His tone makes the hair on the back of my neck stand up. This sounds like a threat and I don't like it one bit.

"What the fuck are you talking about?"

"Just listen to me," he says in a reassuring tone, like he's talking to a cornered animal. "Only I can help you now, everything will be taken care of if you come with me. Come on, let's pick up some of your things and get out of here. I promise I'll take good care of you."

"Casper, no!" I reply horrified. "Let me go!"

"Don't be so stubborn, sweetie," he warns in a harsh voice.

Who is this person? I've never seen him like this.

"I'm not going with you, Casper. I'm staying right here, this is my home."

I'm determined not to give in to him, but I want to know what he's up to, what he's planning.

"I can't believe this, after everything we've been through together, everything I've done for you. Is he all that matters to you? That man? Him? How can you possibly trust him more than me?" Casper has completely lost his mind, he's talking pure nonsense. "You have to believe me, that son of a bitch doesn't deserve you!"

"What are you talking about, Casper?"

I'm playing along with him even though I'd gladly kick him in the nuts and punch his nose, believe me, I know how to do it. But I need answers and I need them right now.

"I know you're a free spirit, Didi," he begins. "No one understands you the way I do. I told Glenn many times that you need a firm hand, but eventually I realized he wasn't the right man for you and so I had to intervene."

My pulse stops. I swear it does.

"What did you do?"

"Come on, Didi, surely you can work it out. Glenn didn't have the strength of character to handle you, or take care of you, he was too soft, so I did you a favor by helping you get away from him."

"How were the slaps I got from him a favor?" I ask incredulously.

"You're too stubborn for your own good. You brought it on yourself." He shrugs, downplaying that horrendous time.

As hard as it is to admit, I have no option but to accept what must have been right there in front of me all along. This friendship has been toxic and unhealthy the entire time.

"Casper, please let me go." Only now do I realize that Casper has gone completely crazy. His friendship has been masking his obsession for me all these years. "Maybe if we talk about this as adults, we can resolve this misunderstanding."

"Well," he says, without letting go of my arm, "we'll talk once I get you away from this filthy place. Let's go to your room and pick up some clothes for you. I'll provide everything else you need, you'll be living like royalty, in a mansion, as you deserve. I don't know why you ever agreed to live with that lowlife."

I just nod as I silently go upstairs to the bedroom, glancing over at the bed as I contemplate what has been our bed for just a brief time.

"And no tricks, Didi," he warns. "I know you too well."

Once in the room, I pick up several things, trying to think of a way to leave some signs that only Adrik will notice, leave him a trail of breadcrumbs.

"Come on, hurry up," Casper urges as he drags me to the closet. "Start packing."

I take out a pair of jeans and a heavy sweater, then my uniform off the hanger. I'm playing for time, looking for an opportunity to land a good blow and make my escape.

Plus I still need some answers.

"I have to admit it was a clever plan." There, I've thrown the bait. "You knew suspicion would immediately fall on Adrik, revenge is always a good motive."

As Casper gives me a creepy, smug smile, I wonder how I could have been so stupid not to have noticed anything was wrong with him before.

"Would you expect anything less from me? Although I must admit it was almost too easy. Getting the key to your apartment wasn't a problem, all it took was a small bribe to the concierge."

"The concierge gave it to you?" *Yes, come on, tell me more, tell me everything.*

I can use Casper's weakness against him, his arrogant pride makes him boastful. He should remember that pride is one of the seven deadly sins.

"Another weak fool, far too easy to manipulate," he laughs. "It's easy if you have money, which I do. For some time I've been lending it to anyone who needs it, at high interest, of course, which has proven to be very profitable. And people pay not only with money, but also with information and favors, it was quite a simple matter to pull a few strings and get that envelope to your father."

Damn him. Damn him a thousand times, I want to cut him up with my own bare hands.

But all in good time.

Calm down, Jordania.

"You're so smart," I praise him. "I've always liked smart guys. Did you install the camera yourself?"

"Sure," he replies. "I didn't want anyone else going in your room. I had to restrain myself knowing that he'd been there… in your bed."

He glares at the bed with disgust and indignation, as if a serious offense has been committed against it.

He sighs and looks at me before adding, "Besides, I couldn't entrust such an important job to just any idiot. If you want something done well, you have to do it yourself, isn't that the philosophy you've always followed? You see, we're compatible in so many ways, my dear Didi."

I close my eyes for a moment, taking a deep breath. I have to keep up the pretense for a little longer, I need to glean more information.

"Why now, Casper? Since you've waited so many years, why not wait a little longer?"

His expression changes, his blue eyes become cloudy.

"I always get what I want, whatever the price. And there is nothing I want more than you. But then Houston came along and swept you up with his lies, his false promises, making you act like a disgusting bitch in heat ever since you met him. How much shit has he put in your head? With every word that comes out of his mouth, I've had to make a huge effort not to throw up on him. I knew that you were planning to live with him in this house, and then I found out that he's having a ring made that he's planning to give you for your birthday."

How the hell did he manage to find out so many things?

This is creepy. Scary.

"I can't understand why you settled for so little?" he continues. *Keep going, Casper, keep talking.* "With a worthless fool like him, you'll get nothing more than cheap trinkets. Don't you understand that you deserve so much better than him? I'm going to treat you like an empress. We'll put all this behind us, forget all about Houston, because now it's just you and me."

This is too much, he is deluded, it's overwhelming.

"Casper, Adrik loves me, he knows how to make me happy."

He shakes me so hard, I hit the wall behind me.

"Nobody loves you as much as I do!" he yells. "Only I can worship you the way you deserve, only I can give you what you need to be happy. Why can't you see this?"

"Casper, I love you, of course I love you," I try to calm him down. "You are my friend, the best in the world, and I care about you so much."

"That's not enough," he exclaims. "You are mine, Didi. You have always been mine, and I've grown tired of standing by and watching while you make mistake after mistake. The time has come for you to realize that I am here for you, to make you see that I'm the man of your dreams."

"How wonderful!" Nothing wonderful about it, Casper it's nuts.

Casper raises his right hand and slaps me and I taste the metallic tang of blood in my mouth.

"Look what you made me do! I didn't want to hurt you, Didi, but you're not listening to reason. I am your savior! You need control, some rules. Although it hurts me to do it, Houston's got you acting like a slut, and that's why you need a man like me to save you from yourself. I already told you, I'm the only one who can truly love you the way you deserve, I am the only one who can give you what you need to be happy."

Who is this crazy, obsessed lunatic?

"I'd rather die than end up in your arms," I yell at him.

Casper has completely lost his mind, so it's now or never.

I kick my leg out and try to hit him in the crotch with all my strength, but he puts a hand there to protect himself. Taking advantage of his vulnerable position, I give him another kick, this time to the ribs, and he collapses in pain.

The bastard deserves it.

Too bad I don't have time to stay and finish him off, but I need to get out of here.

I run downstairs to the living room, but then the heel of my shoe snaps off. I scream in agony as my ankle twists, a reminder of my sprain, however I can't let this stop me as my life is at stake. But when my hair is grabbed from behind, I realize I've lost my opportunity.

"Jordania?" Thank God.

Adrik's here, calling my name as he enters the house, freezing when he sees Casper restraining me.

I am so glad that he's okay, so relieved that he's here for me, and even better, he's not alone.

Out of the corner of my eye, I see a dark-haired man edging along the wall that separates the living room from the kitchen. Zephyr has come with Adrik and is trying to get himself in a better position while Casper's attention is totally focused on Adrik. I don't think he's even noticed the presence of anyone else.

"Well now Houston, you really couldn't have arrived at a better time." Casper smiles coldly at Adrik. "Didi just made an important decision regarding her future. Sweetheart, I'm gonna make your wish come true." When he runs his tongue across my cheek, I nearly vomit in disgust.

That's when I feel the cold metal of a gun slowly sliding up my chest toward my neck, freezing me in place. Casper, my best friend, the man who comforted me in my worst moments and celebrated my triumphs. The man who was always there for me, who stood up for me, is willing to kill me. And I believe he means it, he's not playing games.

When I close my eyes for a moment, all possible scenarios quickly run through my head.

When I open them again, my gaze meets Adrik's, and that's enough to calm me. Without the need for words, I silently convey my determination to him, praying he understands that I have a plan.

Taking a deep breath, I prepare for what's to come. I've never let anyone control me, I have never cowered to anyone and I won't start today. Adrik nods imperceptibly before throwing himself forward.

On reflex, Casper immediately points the weapon at Adrik.

"Keep still, Thunder!" he warns. "She's chosen to die rather than share her life with me, her true love, so I intend to carry out her wish, but not until I've taken care of you first."

"Maybe you should have thought this through better," says an unknown voice, as I feel Casper tense behind me, then hear a trigger being pulled.

"Didi, I wish we'd had more time," Casper moans as he falls to the floor.

And then a heavy silence descends.

Game over.

Rule # 22: Don't be afraid to put her happiness above yours.

Chapter
TWENTY-TWO

I've been pacing round the room at least a thousand times and I can't stop, I'm still fuming.

It's been too much. An intense blow, one that I didn't expect.

I put my trust in someone unworthy, someone who—in his sick mind—thought we were soul mates.

"Everything is ready, Lieutenant," I'm told by the man in front of me. "You can sign your statement now."

Hours later, we find ourselves sitting on uncomfortable plastic chairs in front of a desk in an office at the base command center, complying with the paperwork.

I review the form, paying close attention to every detail. What happened has been really traumatic, as well as painful.

"I still can't believe it," I say to Adrik, who has his hand on my leg. Since we left the house a few hours ago, he hasn't left my side.

"Calm down, my love," he whispers. "In a few moments we'll be out of here, then you can go home and take a nice, relaxing hot bath while I take care of you."

"Adrik, I don't want to go back to the house." So much happened there, I don't have the strength to relive those moments, at least not yet.

"Sorry if I'm intruding, Commander," the officer in charge of internal affairs says. "But we have a hotel at the base. It's nothing fancy, but maybe it would work for you tonight."

"They'll be going to my house," another person intervenes.

Is it really him or am I dreaming it?

"Admiral Zanetti?" I turn around in disbelief. What is my father doing here? And since when does my father own a house in this city?

"Jordania," he says softly, almost fearfully. "If you and Houston need a place to stay, you can use my house for as long as you want to."

"Why would you do that?" I ask skeptically, suspicious of his sudden generosity, especially offering to be Adrik's host.

Have I traveled to an alternate reality?

A parallel world?

I stare at him. I look at my father from head to toe. Is this really him or am I dealing with a well-made replica?

He stares at me and raises his eyebrows. The Admiral knows his words have left my head spinning.

"Because I was wrong and although it's difficult for me to apologize, I must do so, Jordania. It's time for me to recognize that you are an adult, that you know how to lead your life and that you know what's best for you."

Never in my life have I seen him like this, so humble, so vulnerable, and almost human.

"Dad…" I murmur when I find my voice.

My father reaches for my hand and gives it a soft squeeze. He's wrecking me, shocking me with a tenderness that I've never known from him.

"I understand if you and Houston feel uncomfortable staying with me, but the truth is, it's something I hope you'll agree to do to give me some peace of mind." He lets out a sad laughs. "I would just like to know that my only daughter is sleeping safely under my roof, just one last time. It would make your old man happy."

I know how to keep a deck of sailors in order. I've been trained to cope with wars and battle. But this is breaking me, and I have no idea how to cope, especially after what happened tonight.

"I'm not going anywhere without Adrik," I warn him, and I'm serious. Right now I don't think I can take another step if he's not with me.

And if it's true that he's going to respect my decisions, then let him begin by accepting that Adrik and I are together. Forever.

"You're my only daughter and you're making a life with the man you've chosen, so of course Houston is welcome," he says. "My house is open to both of you, unconditionally."

And with that, there's nothing more to be said.

Before I can think through, I jump into my father's arms. At first, the poor man is shocked—to be honest, so am I. I've just thrown us both for a loop—but after a few awkward seconds, he hugs me back. Hard.

I know that it's hard for him to say what's in his heart. I've been there. We are people of action.

"Your mother would be so proud of you, my child."

Tonight my father seems determined to knock me over.

"You never talk about her, Daddy."

"We will, my brown-eyed girl, we will." I'm floating on a cloud, my feet aren't touching the ground, and it isn't because my father is lifting me up.

Glancing up from my father's shoulder, I find Adrik's smoky gaze on me.

And he's smiling.

Broadly.

Hours later, we are lying together on my father's guest bed, unable to fall asleep after everything that happened.

"How did you get released so quickly?" I ask. "Casper told me that you had been arrested."

He takes a deep breath before answering. "They didn't have any proof against me, and it didn't take long for them to work out that I would have come out as badly as you with the publication of those photos. I'm a highly respected officer with an unblemished record and a good reputation. I'm well regarded around here." Adrik sighs, his body as exhausted as mine, but neither of us can sleep a wink.

There is too much to talk about, so much to say.

"Everyone knows about us at the base, it's no secret. Zephyr called Benson for me, he's a lawyer friend with the right contacts, and he took care of everything."

Thank God for connections and good friends, this mess would have been much more complicated to sort without them, and I can't bear the thought of Adrik in a military jail...

"Do you think Casper will manage to dodge what's coming?"

He laughs sourly.

"No, love, he won't," he states firmly. "Your friend will be put behind bars for a long time. His crimes are pretty serious, and not even the best lawyer is going to be able to help him. I'll make sure of that."

"He's not my friend, at least not anymore."

A part of me—just a small part—is sad about the friend I lost, although at this point I have to admit that he never was. It gives me the creeps just to think how the loving friend I thought I knew was just the act of an obsessive madman.

And speaking of obsession…

"Adrik," I say, crawling over his chest to look him in the eye. "Casper was determined to end the life we had planned out for us."

"Damn man," he grumbles. "He doesn't know what is waiting for him. I don't care what I have to do, but I am going to make sure he has a speedy recovery so he can start his new life in jail as soon as possible. Your father agrees with me."

Holy crap, should I start worrying about this new alliance?

"Adrik, I've no idea how, but Casper knew you were having a ring made for me."

He grabs my ass and flips me over.

"Fucking interfering bastard, I can say goodbye to my surprise." He shakes his head before sighing. "I know your birthday is approaching, so I ordered a ring, it was going to be your present."

Could my heart burst again? This time with happiness?

"I've thinking about this long and hard. When I asked you to move in with me, it was because deep in my soul I knew you were the one. You are the only woman for me, Jordania."

"Thank you for going to so much trouble to make it special, you know it wasn't necessary."

He looks at me seriously, holding my face with both his hands.

"My love, I know you'd settle for a ring from a cereal box, but I want only the best for you. I want you to be proud to wear my ring for the rest of your life."

Where has Commander Thunder gone?

This man is being so sweet, he's about to make me cry.

"I'm already so proud of you, Adrik, and I would be honored to be your wife."

He is the only thing I need.

Suddenly, he bolts off the bed like a streak of lightning and begins looking through his clothes for something.

"What the heck are you doing?" I ask, thinking he's acting very weird. "Adrik, you're scaring me, what are you doing?"

"I need my phone, damn it, where did I leave it?"

His phone?

Who does he need to call so urgently at this time?

"What's up, Adrik?"

"Now that it's actually happening, now that you said yes, I don't want to wait any longer. I'm going to book a flight right now, you and I are going to Las Vegas, tonight you're going to be legally mine. Did I mention we're going tonight?"

He keeps looking until he finds it, then presses the screen as he starts searching.

"Adrik, you do realize you haven't actually asked me yet? And I'm kinda looking forward to a formal proposal, sir."

That immediately stops him in his tracks, surprised by my reaction.

"Don't you want to marry me?"

I laugh softly at his horrified expression. "I'm just saying that what I'd like is for you to *ask* me, you know?"

This is only going to happen once, right? I plan on my marriage lasting a lifetime. No, that's too short, forever sounds better.

Adrik approaches the bed, still clutching his phone, until he's leaning right over me.

"Jordania Marie Zanetti, do you want to escape to Las Vegas right now so that I can make you my wife?"

"I can't get married in Vegas, Commander, I want all my Pinterest wedding board dreams to come true."

Oh my... the face he just made.

"You don't even have a Pinterest account."

True, why does this damn man have to be so smart?

"Maybe I don't, but it was worth pretending just to see your face."

"Let's get hitched then."

"Oh no, Houston, not so fast. I have a better idea."

I get up from the bed and start to get ready.

"You're so bossy," he tells me.

Yes, I am, but he loves me anyway.

"Don't you know? I'm not bossy, I am The Boss."

The next morning at about eleven, we're boarding a flight to paradise. We're going to Kauai, the place where our story began, and where Adrik and I will soon become husband and wife.

"That's not soon enough," he'd grumbled, on learning he'd have to wait a little.

"Maybe I can come up with some suggestions on how to pass the time. I know what you like, Houston." I'd winked, and it proved easy enough to convince him. He certainly wasn't complaining when some hours later he'd held me in his arms, sweaty, satisfied, and completely happy.

I'm going to be his wife, I can't believe it, but now I have the ring to prove it dazzling on my finger.

"I thought you didn't care about the ring," he'd commented, when he realized I was staring at it for the umpteenth time that day.

"That was before I found out how gorgeous it was."

It is a truly beautiful ring, three rectangular stones, the largest in the middle, flanked by two smaller ones. According to Adrik, it is an art deco design. I think it's gorgeous—a beautiful picture of our relationship—and I never want to take it off my hand.

With the help of a very efficient wedding planner, we have everything set for our big moment. Flowers, pictures, and even a beautiful cake. The girl knows her business, in twenty four hours she organized it all to what can only be rival to a precise military operation.

"Are you ready, Miss Zanetti?" Brittany, the planner asks, before opening the glass doors leading to the beach.

This is the last time someone calls me by my maiden name. Next time I'll be Mrs. Adrik Houston. Can you believe it?

"I'm ready." I smile, knowing that Adrik will be there, waiting for me.

I walk barefoot, in a simple white satin dress that I bought earlier in a vintage boutique near the hotel. I'm holding a bouquet of white orchids to complete the look, and I'm wearing my hair loose, cascading down my back, held by a flower on the side of my head. Just as my fiancé likes it.

I don't need anything else, everything I want is waiting for me just a few steps away wearing a beige linen suit.

Our eyes meet and everything else disappears, there's just the sunset and us.

The way he smiles at me overshadows the orange reflections on the horizon. He is my light, shining out to me.

This is really happening. We have a future, a life together, and it's going to be exciting and unpredictable.

And all ours.

The time to wander alone is over, now that he is by my side. Forever and always. He and I.

Adrik

My Adrik... my lighting and thunder. My very own storm.

"Is this what you wanted?" he asks, kissing my neck in the way that I like so much.

"Everything I could possibly want and more," I answer, as desire overwhelms me.

"My wife," he whispers. "My beautiful wife."

Ah, how wonderful that sounds.

Our spirits are water and fire combined, like these beautiful islands.

The love we share completes everything, sets our world into motion, and is the force that drives us to live.

I thought my life was about achievement and success.

I had to fight for that, and then I had to fight for this as well.

And I'm proud to say, I believed I could, so I did.

Epilogue

"This means waaaaar." When I hear a shriek from the end of my bed, I close my eyes and try to ignore it.

But it soon proves to be an impossible task.

"Fight, fight, fight…" says another little voice, ready to battle.

God, it's not even six in the morning. Welcome to our wonderful life.

"More screaming, huh?" Adrik murmurs, before stroking my neck with his nose.

"What better way to start the day," I reply wryly. "We should be used to it by now."

But it's never easy.

"I'm getting up, you stay in bed a little longer."

He doesn't have to tell me twice. The long-awaited weekend has finally arrived, and a few minutes of extra rest is just what the doctor ordered.

Twelve years have passed since we said yes in that magical sunset. Twelve years full of fights, reconciliations, challenges, and conquests, but, above all, twelve years full of love.

"I'm not getting any younger," I told my husband one night a few years back, as we lay naked in bed after making love.

"I have no idea what you're talking about," he replied, his hands wandering over my back.

"My biological clock is ticking," I clarified. Men never get these things, or maybe they just prefer to act dumb. "If you want to fill the house with children, it's about time we start."

"And here I was thinking this moment would be tearful and romantic," he teased me. "If you're asking me for a baby, you better start sending me flowers."

"This is serious, Thunder. I'm worried that if we wait any longer, it'll be too late."

"My love," he said, kissing my hair. "In case you haven't heard, science is making great technological advancements, meaning we don't have to make a hasty decision just because of the pressure of time."

"But what if we find out too late that we can't?"

His laugh irritated and comforted me at the same time. Some things never change.

"If we can't, we'll find another way."

"But I know how much you want a family," I worried, having seen the way he loved playing with our friends' children, knowing that he'd made such a great father, the way he was so loving and patient.

"Jordania, you are my family," he said, sliding his hand around my waist as he moved to align his body with mine. "Everything I need is here."

His tender words filled my eyes with tears.

"But Adrik, I want to have your children. I want to make babies with you."

His eyes widened in surprise, then seconds later his mouth was plundering mine.

"Adrik…" I murmured, our conversation was not finished.

"My wife wants a baby, her wish is my command."

"What about my pills?" I asked. "I've been taking them religiously for years."

"Forget about them, put them in the trash," he murmured between kisses.

So I did what he said. The pills were forgotten, along with everything else when his body invaded mine.

Three months later he kept shaking his head in disbelief as the word "pregnant" appeared on the pregnancy test we'd bought.

A few months later, Aria and Luana Houston announced their arrival to the world, screaming their dark-haired heads off. Six years have passed and nothing much has changed, they still love to be loud.

Two years after our girls were born, I got a nasty intestinal bug. Long story short, that bug meant my pills failed and I ended up pregnant again. Tristan, the baby of the family, arrived months later. It was unexpected, and it certainly made our life a little more complicated, but it has also brought so much happiness.

I can say with confidence that my little warriors possess the strongest will I've ever known, after experiencing six years of their energetic willfulness and stubbornness. They are also little lightning bolts, who don't stop for a single minute, playing and jumping around until I'm about to drop from sheer exhaustion.

Well what did I expect?

No, it's nothing like in a fairytale. Adrik and I are strong, bossy and restless, so why would our children be any different?

You know what? I wouldn't change them for anything in the world. Not for anything or anyone.

They are just perfect the way they are.

"Mommy," a little voice whispers as the door to our room opens wide. "What time are you going to wake up? Dad is in the kitchen with Aria and Luana, and I'm bored."

Adrik's an adoring father and our daughters are complete Daddy's girls, but Tristan is the consummate Momma's boy.

"What does my boy want to do today?"

The big smile on my little man's face could light up the entire city.

"Can we play in the garden?"

I never have the willpower to say no to my sweet boy.

Half an hour later, all five of us are sitting around the kitchen table eating breakfast. Nothing has changed in our routine, Adrik is still in charge of the menu while I sip coffee from my beloved pineapple cup—yes, the one he gave me that day in Kauai.

"What time is Ganpa coming?" Luana asks. The three of them nod excitedly, they can't wait to see their grandfather.

Yes, that's right, their grandfather, as in my father. After everything that happened with Casper and those photos, something changed in him. He was never quite the same again and neither was our relationship. It was as if a dam broke, unleashing a totally different person. Shortly after we announced my pregnancy, my father declared that he was ready to retire.

To say that we were speechless was an understatement.

"It's time for me to enjoy my family," he said, and family included Adrik's grandparents too.

Luana and Adair now are living in an assisted living facility, that my father helped us find using his connections. After meeting them, he also became very fond of them. We visit them at least twice a week, kids included.

"I want to be involved and to play with my grandchildren while I still can," he added and with that, we acquired the best nanny the world has ever known.

We've often heard him say that being called grandfather is how he likes to be known, the proud and revered title of admiral has been left behind. My children can twist him around their little fingers, and he is more than happy with that.

We've all made mistakes, but they are in the past and we've forgiven, forgotten, and moved on. Family is the most important thing, after all, and its love that binds us all together.

Yes, now I'm the one throwing out the cheesy lines here and there. I've also changed over the years. Not too much though.

I'm still working, but here on the mainland now. Recently, as part of the modernization of the naval base, a new department was opened for the development of new technologies, and guess who is in charge.

Yes, you got it! Me!

All of those things I learned in the field and during training are now helping me to develop new combat technologies. My name is well-known around the world, I've worked with several countries, just last month I came back from Japan. The Navy sent me in a commission to evaluate an all-terrain vehicle the Japanese are developing; the thing is like a mechanical horse and will be amazing for missions in uneven terrain, like the South American jungle. It needs some hydraulics adjustments, but soon enough we will be manufacturing a new version of it here in the US, generating tons of new jobs.

Now I am Commander Jordania Zanetti-Houston. Adrik stole my heart, so in return I took his last name. Adrik's a captain now, and the rumor is that he will soon be promoted to rear admiral, I'm so fucking proud of my husband; we are the personification of a power couple, after all.

"Who is ready to go on vacation?" Adrik yells at the children, who immediately begin jumping around as if possessed.

Just seeing them like this makes me so happy, my heart skips a beat.

"Mommy, Ganpa said that we can eat all the sweets we want," Aria exclaims, her smoky eyes bright with emotion.

"Luckily," Adrik intervenes in a rather mocking tone, "he's the one who's going to have to deal with the consequences."

In a few hours, my father will take the children to spend a few days in Florida. According to him, they've already been too many times to the California Park and a change of locale is needed. With that, he's given us the perfect excuse to escape for a few days to our refuge.

Yes, I still have that little house in Kauai, and we escape there whenever we can. Unfortunately that doesn't happen as often as we would like as our work is very demanding and the children must go to school.

"Happy?" he asks, while making sure my seat belt is on, protective like always.

Come on, is not as if we're paragliding, and this is a latest generation aircraft.

"Are you happy, Jordania?" It's incredible that after so many years, he still asks the same thing.

"More than happy, Captain," I whisper, my lips glued to his.

"Any regrets?"

"Yes," I answer. "Not tying you up with one of the ropes on the tree the day we met."

"Ah, but you did, love," he corrects me. "From that moment on, I was completely yours."

"Really?"

"You still have doubts?"

His hand leads mine to where his pants are doing little to hide the obvious.

"I think you're suffering from Priapus, Houston."

"No, ma'am," he corrects me. "I'm suffering from the incurable illness of being crazy about you."

"Too bad we still have more than five hours of flight left."

We only just took off.

"Flying first class has its advantages, especially if my wife is wearing a skirt. Jordania, are you ready for me? Shall I see what I can do to torture you just a little bit?"

I have been ready ever since I met him, because as he just said, that day under the tree we sealed our destiny. We embarked on an adventure together, one that I hope will never end.

A circle of love and happiness.

My father was right. I wasn't born to be average. I'm one in a million, so is our love.

People fight the storm, but I embrace it, because the storm and I are one.

The End

About the Author

Susana Mohel is a USA Today best-selling author whose stories sizzle like the sunshine in her Southern California mountains.

Her fast-paced, angsty contemporary romance novels transport readers to a world of spunky heroines and hunky heroes who find their way to a happily ever after… with plenty of spiced-up moments along the way.

When she's not writing, Susana can be found wandering the trails along with her husband or creating chaos in her garden.

www.susanamohel.com